# SKYE, THE JURY

The night before, the brown-haired girl had come to Skye Fargo's bedroom to passionately plead her cause. Now tonight there was a knocking on his door again, and a voice whispering, "May I come in?"

Skye didn't bother pulling the sheet up over his naked body when he answered, "It's open." The girl had already seen all of him there was to see.

But this was a different girl. The black-haired one.

"I want you to believe in me," she said.

"Sorry," Fargo said. "I'm not figuring to talk about your proof of identity anymore."

"Neither am I," the girl said, and drew her nightgown up over her head to reveal the delightful curves and delicious ripeness of her body.

*Skye had to decide which one of the girls was telling the truth about herself. He felt duty-bound to explore all the evidence. . . .*

# THE TRAILSMAN
## 57

# FORTUNE
# RIDERS

by

## Jon Sharpe

A SIGNET BOOK

NEW AMERICAN LIBRARY

*PUBLISHER'S NOTE*

This novel is a work of fiction. Names, characters, places, and incidents either are the product of the author's imagination or are used fictitiously, and any resemblance to actual persons, living or dead, events, or locales is entirely coincidental.

The first chapter of this book previously appeared in *Guns of Hungry Horse*, the fifty-sixth volume in this series.

SIGNET TRADEMARK REG. U.S. PAT. OFF. AND FOREIGN COUNTRIES
REGISTERED TRADEMARK—MARCA REGISTRADA
HECHO EN CHICAGO, U.S.A.

SIGNET, SIGNET CLASSIC, MENTOR, ONYX, PLUME, MERIDIAN AND NAL BOOKS are published by New American Library, 1633 Broadway, New York, New York 10019

First Printing, September, 1986

1  2  3  4  5  6  7  8  9

PRINTED IN THE UNITED STATES OF AMERICA

# The Trailsman

Beginnings . . . they bend the tree and they
mark the man. Skye Fargo was born when
he was eighteen. Terror was his midwife,
vengeance his first cry. Killing spawned
Skye Fargo, ruthless, cold-blooded murder.
Out of the acrid smoke of gunpowder still
hanging in the air, he rose, cried out a
promise never forgotten.

The Trailsman, they began to call him,
all across the West: searcher, scout, hunter,
the man who could see where others only
looked, his skills for hire but not his soul,
the man who lived each day to the fullest,
yet trailed each tomorrow. Skye Fargo,
the Trailsman, the seeker who could take
the wildness of a land and the wanting
of a woman and make them his own.

*Missouri, 1860,*
*state of compromise and controversy,*
*where death and deceit were as common*
*as a copper penny . . .*

## 1

Trouble!

The big man with the lake-blue eyes spat the word silently.

Trouble, he repeated to himself.

He saw it instantly, in the very way the stagecoach roared into town, in the set of the driver's jaw, in the way he reined up in front of the depot. The big man rose to his feet and grimaced. He'd been waiting for the four-o'clock stage, and now it rolled in late and the whole thing spelled trouble. Damn, he muttered inwardly.

The stage was a poor-man's Concord, he noted, a reinforced mud-wagon with open sides hung with narrow strips of isinglass, and it skittered sideways as the driver brought the two-horse team to a halt. The front platform of a feed store served as the stage depot and the storekeeper as depot master. Fargo saw the man hurry from his store, concern on his face.

"Got dry-gulched," the driver called to him as he swung from the stage.

"Where?" another voice cut in, and Fargo saw a

man with a long, narrow face and a body to match step forward, a sheriff's badge on his frayed shirt.

"Right at Three Forks Bend, Sheriff," the driver answered.

"Anybody hurt?" the sheriff queried.

"They took a girl that was aboard," the driver said. "Dragged her out and took off with her."

Fargo flicked a glance at the sheriff and saw the man quickly put on a frown of dismay that had an air of caution in it. "Reckon they're long gone by now," the sheriff murmured.

Fargo kept the derisive grunt inside himself, flicked a glance edged with contempt at the man, and returned his eyes to the stage as two men stepped out. Both were well-dressed, in frock coats. Both were in their early fifties, he guessed. The sheriff made no move to do anything but look pained, Fargo saw as he stepped out to where the two men were taking their bags from the rear compartment of the stage. The ambush certainly wasn't his business, and he wasn't about to make it so.

"Which of you gents is P. J. Peabody?" he asked, and both men turned to frown back at him.

"Not me," the one said.

"Me neither," the other answered. "But that was the name of the gal those dry-gulchers dragged off the stage."

Fargo felt the frown slide across his brow. "Her name was P. J. Peabody?" he asked.

"Penelope Julia Peabody, she called herself. Got to talking with her. Came aboard back in Arkansas," the man said.

Fargo muttered a silent curse, and the letter inside his jacket pocket suddenly seemed to throb. Trouble

had turned around and become his. With the suddenness of a peregrine falcon's dive it had become his.

"Where's this Three Forks Bend?" he shot at the
stage driver.

"Just follow the road and you'll reach it in a few
miles," the man said.

Fargo turned, strode to the Ovaro tethered nearby,
and felt the sheriff's eyes follow him.

"What's this to you, mister?" the sheriff called out.

"Don't know yet, but I was waiting to meet P. J.
Peabody on that stage. Didn't know it'd be a girl,
though," Fargo said as he climbed onto the magnifi-
cent horse with the jet black fore and hindquarters
and the glistening white midsection.

"It's too late. You can't pick up their trail now," the
sheriff said.

"Maybe you can't," Fargo tossed back as he sent
the Ovaro into a fast canter, his mouth a thin line.

The dry-gulchers had taken more than a girl by the
name of P. J. Peabody from the stage. They'd taken
the promise of a thousand dollars from him, to say
nothing of the monies he'd turned down to be here,
and that made trouble a very personal thing.

He sent the Ovaro down the wide main street of
town, skirted a big, slow-moving platform spring
dray loaded with iron ore and limestone, and
threaded his way through the crowded street.

Otisville was a gateway town, sitting astride the
ore-mining country to its north, the hog and cattle
land to its south, and the pathway west into the
Kansas Territory. A town growing too fast for itself.
Fargo was glad to reach the end of its crowded, noisy
main street and race the Ovaro onto the dirt road with
a growth of tall sugar maples on both sides.

The road became a winding path that rose into low hill country, and Fargo swore silently as he saw the daylight beginning to slide toward dusk. He rode hard and the hills grew higher alongside the road. Three Forks Bend was plain enough to spot when he reached it, three smaller paths branching out from a sharp bend in the road. He reined to a halt. The ground was a crumbled, torn bed of ruts and marks, but he scanned the bend with eyes that read where other men only saw, his eyes the Trailsman's eyes. He noted each sign, mark, print, and indentation, each a message of its own, and he put them together the way ordinary men put together words to make a sentence.

The girl had fought them, and they'd had to drag her from the stage to the other side of the bend, he saw. His eyes narrowed in concentration. They'd gone on back the way the stage had come, turned off the road onto a gentle slope of hill almost at once. Four, maybe five horses, he grunted as he followed the tracks, the heavy growth of downy bromegrass making it hard to be exact. He hurried, his eyes fixed on the trail, which disappeared in places and came up yards farther on. A small side road opened up between a stand of thick serviceberry shrubs. He slowed, squinted along the pathway, and continued on past. The heavy bromegrass suddenly thinned, and he grunted in satisfaction as the tracks became clear again.

He'd just sent the Ovaro into the narrow pathway the tracks took northward when the shot exploded through the gathering dusk. Fargo felt the rush of air as the bullet all but grazed his head. He toppled sideways from the horse, hit the ground hard, and lay motionless. But his mind raced as he cursed at his own mistakes. He'd been racing to beat the fading light, concentrating too hard on the tracks he followed. He hadn't expected the unexpected—always a mistake. The dry-gulchers hadn't been entirely unconcerned about being followed. Obviously, they'd left a rifleman to wait and watch.

Fargo remained motionless on the ground, his eyes only tiny slitted openings. He could see only a narrow area in front of him and so he let his ears fill in the rest as he picked up the sound of a horse's hooves moving slowly down the slope. He remained motionless, certain the rider would still have the rifle trained on him.

The sound of the horse's footsteps drew closer, and he heard the faint rattle of rein chains, then the soft, brushed sound of leather against leather as the rider swung from the saddle. Fargo stayed unmoving, holding his breath. Through eyes that appeared closed, he saw the boots come into his narrow line of vision. The boots moved closer, and Fargo saw the long barrel of the rifle as the man halted beside him. He continued to hold his breath, thoughts racing wildly through his mind. There'd be but one chance, he knew, one, single, split-second instant. He had to seize the exact moment or take the full blast of the rifle at point-blank range.

He felt the man's boot dig into his side, lift, and turn him onto his back. He kept his body lifelessly limp while he swore inwardly. He couldn't even tense his muscles to be ready for that fleeting moment. The man leaned over him, reached down, and Fargo felt more than saw him pull the big Colt free. But through the narrow perimeter of his all-but-closed eyes he saw the mouth of the rifle barrel lift and tilt away from him for an instant as the man bent over. Fargo drove his leg forward and up with all the strength of calf and thigh muscles and caught the man right behind one knee. The figure went backward and down. Fargo felt the hot blast as the rifle fired into the air just past his ear, and he flung himself sideways, slammed into the man as he struggled to regain his feet. The blow knocked the dry-gulcher back and sent both the rifle and the Colt flying out of his hands.

Fargo leapt to his feet and saw a short, thick-waisted figure with a face as puffy as his body. The man reached for his own gun, and Fargo twisted his body as he kicked out and his foot sank into the man's belly.

"Shit," the man gasped as he doubled half over in pain. He pulled at his gun again, but the rhythm and speed of his draw had been broken. Fargo dived, closed one big hand around the man's wrist as the six-gun cleared the holster.

"Son of a bitch," the man cursed as he went back and followed with a grunt of pain as Fargo twisted his wrist and the gun fell from his fingers. The dry-gulcher brought his legs up together and aimed for the big man's stomach with his knees but Fargo rolled away. The short, thick figure went onto its side and came up just in time to take a whistling left hook Fargo threw from one knee. The blow came in a little high and landed on the man's mouth. A spurt of blood reddened the left corner of his face as the man went backward.

"Goddamn bastard," the man snarled, and he lunged forward. Fargo, on his feet now, threw another left hook and saw it strike only thin air as the man swerved almost at right angles in the middle of his lunge.

"Damn," Fargo spit out, for he saw the reason as the thick figure dived for the six-gun on the ground nearby. The man reached it, got his hand around the weapon, rolled, and started to bring it up to fire.

Fargo's leap had the speed, power, and spearing accuracy of a cougar diving on its prey. His forearm smashed down onto the man's throat as he landed, and he heard the small neck vertebrae splinter, a sound not unlike that of tiny twigs being cracked. The man's finger tightening on the trigger was a reflex action, and the shot went wild as the gun fell from his hand. A stream of red bubbles spilled from the dry-gulcher's mouth and a harsh, wheezing sound only brought up more scarlet. Fargo pushed away and the puffy face became a mask of contortion. The man's thick body jerked violently for an instant and lay still. Dusk gave way to night and life to death.

Fargo rose, his mouth a thin line. The dry-gulcher would answer no questions, and Fargo retrieved his Colt and walked to the Ovaro. The night made following tracks impossible and he drew upon something else: that undefinable ability called trail sense—part reason, part experience, part law of averages, and part sixth sense.

The trail had followed along the bottom of the slope, paralleled a line of spiny-leafed black oak, and Fargo sent the Ovaro on along the same course in the new night. He let the terrain guide him, followed the curves and rises that unfolded, and climbed onto a low ridge that came easily to his path. He slowed as his nostrils caught the unmistakable scent of woodsmoke, and he turned the horse as he followed the scent. He moved down slowly and caught the faint glow of light through the darkness. He moved through a thick growth of oak and slowed again as a little hollow came into sight. A cabin took shape as he moved closer, the smoke spiraling from its low chimney. Fargo halted inside the oaks and surveyed the hollow of land and took in the four horses tethered to a low branch off to one side of the open land.

He dismounted and left the Ovaro in a deep thicket of trees, started down to the hollow and the little cabin. Moving into a crouch as he emerged into the hollow, he heard voices from inside the cabin and a sharp half-scream of pain. The cabin, a ramshackle affair with the door hanging half off its hinges, sported a side window. He stayed low as he reached it, lifted his head just enough to let him peer over the rough-cut length of log that served as a windowsill. He took in the scene inside in one sweeping glance. The cabin was a one-room affair, the girl on the floor, a long-haired man holding her arms behind her, three others looking on. They'd lighted a fire more for light than warmth, and Fargo let his eyes stay on the girl. She had brown, curly hair and brown eyes that tried to look defiant through their fear. All in all, it was an even-featured face, more pleasant than striking. A high-button tan dress had the top buttons torn open, and a curve of modest breasts rose into sight.

Fargo brought his eyes to the four men as one tossed another piece of wood into the fireplace. A smallish figure, he walked with a strange, quick gait, something between a limp and a hop. "Well, if we're goin' to enjoy her first, let's get to it," he muttered as the firelight flared.

"No rush," the long-haired one holding the girl said, an oily anticipation in his voice. "We can keep her here all week for ourselves."

"Don't like it," one of the others put in, a man wearing a red-checkered shirt. "The boss said just to get rid of her."

"He won't even know," the long-haired one said. "Since when did you get so quick to turn down a piece of ass, Charley?"

"All right, all right," the one called Charley muttered. "But it's my ass I'm thinking about. You know how mad the boss can get."

The fourth man spoke up, and Fargo saw an almost toothless grin break open a flat face with a pushed-in nose. "Then you just stand by and watch, Charley," the man said. "You can count how many times I bang her." He stepped toward the girl as he started to unbutton Levi's.

Fargo watched the girl try to kick at him, but the long-haired one holding her pulled on her arms and she cried out in pain.

"Bastards. You leave me alone," she flung out.

Fargo's glance swept the cabin again. He discarded the thought of bursting in through the door. The four dry-gulchers were spaced too far apart. He could bring down two, maybe three at best, before he took a fusillade of hot lead. Besides, a shoot-out in the little cabin could easily send a stray bullet into the girl. He stayed crouched as he backed away from the window, his mind racing. He had to get the men out of the cabin where he could have the advantage of position.

"Hold her damn legs," someone shouted inside the cabin.

Fargo cursed silently; he had damn little time to act. He swept the hollow of land with his eyes and brought his gaze back to the ramshackle cabin. He watched the spiral of smoke drift up from the low chimney. Suddenly he was running on silent footsteps, racing around to the rear of the cabin. He heard the sound of a hard slap and the girl's cry of pain as he reached the rear of the cabin where the roof dipped low. He halted, bent his knees, knotted powerful calf and thigh muscles, and leapt up. He felt his hands catch hold on the uneven roof logs, and he hung there for a moment before beginning to pull his long, power-packed frame up and over. Once on the roof, he crawled up on hands and knees until he reached the chimney. Pulling his jacket off, Fargo spread it across the top of the chimney to effectively close the opening.

He crouched beside the chimney with a clear view of the ground below, the big Colt in his hand. The smoke would collect itself for a few moments, then come billowing out of the fireplace on a back draft to fill the cabin with its choking clouds. Fargo had counted off a little more than thirty seconds when he heard the curses mixed with coughs and the figures stumbled from the cabin into the fresh air. He waited until he saw the girl. She crawled on her stomach, a billow of smoke rolling over her.

"Drop your guns and nobody gets hurt," Fargo called down. The choking, coughing figures froze for a moment, then turned to squint up at the cabin roof. The long-haired one and the man called Charley were closest below him, Fargo noted. "Drop your guns," he ordered again.

"Shit," the long-haired man cursed as he yanked at his gun. Fargo's Colt barked instantly and the bullet slammed into the man from above, drove downward through the top of his skull. His head split down the center and he seemed to collapse to the ground in two sections. Fargo shifted the big Colt, fired again before the second man could bring his gun up, and the figure spun completely around before it fell. The other two had seized the chance to run for the horses, and Fargo aimed at the dim shapes as they ran across the hollow. He fired again and saw one racing figure pitch face forward to the ground. The fourth man had reached the horses in the darkness at the edge of the hollow, and Fargo heard the sound of a horse galloping away.

Fargo rose, pulled his jacket from the chimney, slipped it on, and lowered himself over the front edge of the roof. He landed a few feet from the girl and saw her stare at him as she wiped the last of the smoke from her eyes. He glanced across the ground at the third man and saw it was the one they'd called Charley. That left the little man with the strange hoplike gait as the one that got away, Fargo noted. Then he turned his eyes back to the girl, reached down, and pulled her to her feet.

"Let's go inside," he said. "The smoke's cleared away by now."

She pulled the top of her dress closed as she walked beside him and a tiny frown furrowed her brow as she peered at him.

Inside the cabin, she turned to face him, and he had the chance to take her in properly for the first time. She was, he saw, one of those girls he referred to as nicely medium—girls that had nothing outstanding about them, nothing striking, no single, exciting feature, no special spark, yet they were not unattractive. She fitted: medium height, medium brown hair, medium brown eyes, a medium figure, and a medium bustline. Everything nicely medium, he grunted inwardly.

"Thank you," she said. "It sounds so inadequate. They planned to kill me."

"Eventually," Fargo said, and she nodded grimly.

"I guess this is my lucky night," she said.

"Lucky?" He frowned.

"That you happened by," she said.

"I didn't just happen by," Fargo said, and it was her turn to frown. "I was there when the stage pulled into town. I came after you when I heard what happened."

"Then I'm doubly grateful," she said. "Very few men would have done that."

"Had a reason. The name's Fargo . . . Skye Fargo," he said.

"Well, Skye Fargo, I'll never be able to thank you for what you did," the girl said, and Fargo peered hard at her. There was no mistaking the gratefulness in her eyes, but there was nothing else, not even the flicker of anything else.

"Who are you?" He frowned.

"Penelope Julia Peabody," she said.

"The hell you are," Fargo snapped.

"I beg your pardon," she said in surprise.

"You're not P. J. Peabody," Fargo snapped.

"Of course I am," she retorted. "Why do you say that?"

"Because my name didn't mean a damn thing to you," Fargo said. "How come, seeing as how P. J. Peabody sent me a letter, which I have in my pocket?"

Her lips fell open for a moment, but she pulled them closed quickly. "I didn't send you a letter," she said.

"But you're P. J. Peabody?" Fargo pressed.

"I am," she said, a touch of asperity coming into her voice.

"Bullshit, honey," Fargo said quietly. "But I aim to find out who you are."

## 2

"I am Penelope Julia Peabody," the girl repeated, and Fargo saw a line of determined strength creep across her lips that was definitely more than medium in character.

"Who were those dry-gulchers?" he asked.

"I don't know," she said.

"Why were they after you?" he barked.

"I don't know."

"Who sent me that letter?"

"I don't know."

"Why would anybody send me a letter signed P. J. Peabody?" Fargo pressed.

"I don't know," she said.

"Seems you don't know a hell of a lot for having come all the way out here," he tossed at her.

"I know I'm Penelope Julia Peabody," the girl said, and he saw the doggedness come into her brown eyes.

"And I know something stinks," he snapped. "Can you ride?"

"Of course," she said with annoyance.

"Use one of their horses. I'll take you back to town. You can use the time to tell me why you're out here. We'll start there," he said roughly.

"Fine. I've no secrets," she said.

His short grunt was a derisive sound as he watched her climb onto one of the horses and come over to where he waited on the Ovaro. She had a trim, compact shape, he noted as she rode beside him, no loose sway at all to her modest breasts.

"Talk," he growled.

"I'm here to claim my father's estate," Penelope began. "I received a letter saying there might be a great deal of money waiting for me if I appeared in person to claim the estate."

"What estate?"

"The Peabody Mining Company, according to the letter. I don't really know anything much about this. The letter came as a complete surprise. I never knew my father was alive," she said, and Fargo frowned back. "I never knew him, never saw him, didn't even know who he was until the letter came," she said.

"Your ma never told you anything?"

"No, she raised me back in Tennessee, and when she died, I moved in with a friend in Arkansas. My father simply didn't exist for me," Penelope said.

"Until you got this letter from him," Fargo said, and she nodded.

"Who else knew you were coming out here?" Fargo asked.

"I was told to write the manager of the mine if I was coming, a Mike Shaw. Maybe he told a lot of people. I don't know," the girl said.

"Maybe. Somebody knew and didn't want you on the scene," Fargo said.

"Yes, and I don't understand any of it." The girl frowned and seemed honestly confused.

Fargo turned what she'd said in his mind. It was all very neat and convenient, a letter out of the blue offering a sudden inheritance, an heiress nobody knew existed. It told him very little and actually answered nothing and sure as hell didn't shed any light on the letter he'd received. He put it away in a corner of his mind for the moment.

"You have that letter with you?" he asked.

"It was in my bag on the stage," Penelope said.

"I'd guess your things were left at the stage depot. We'll pick them up," Fargo said as Otisville took shape through the darkness. He rode through the now quiet main street of the town and halted before the darkened depot. A light burned on the second floor of the feed store, and Fargo dismounted, pounded on the door until footsteps clumped down a stairway inside. The door opened and Fargo saw the storekeeper–depot master stare at him. Then the man's eyes went to Penelope.

"You have the lady's bag?" Fargo asked.

"My God, you found her," the man said in amazement.

"The bag," Fargo said.

"Yes, got it right here," the man said, and pulled a traveling bag from a wood rack. He handed it up to Penelope, who took it with a grateful nod. "Wait here a minute, mister. Let me get Sheriff Hazer. He'll want to know. He'll be real glad," the depot master said.

"And real surprised," Fargo said, but he stayed as the man hurried down the street a dozen yards, pounded on a door, and returned in moments with the sheriff's narrow frame hurrying beside him.

The sheriff took in Penelope first, then his eyes went to the big man in front of him. "You did real well. Who are you, mister?" the sheriff asked.

"Name's Fargo. Some call me the Trailsman," Skye said.

Sheriff Hazer's eyes narrowed a fraction. "I've heard of you," he said. "Who were they?"

"Didn't have time to ask. You don't really care, do you?" Fargo said.

"What's that mean?" The sheriff frowned.

"You could've gone after them," Fargo said.

"I figured it was a waste of time," the sheriff said.

"Try again," Fargo grunted.

"What are you sayin', Fargo?" Sheriff Hazer flared.

"Either you're a coward or just lazy, or you know when to look the other way. Or maybe all three, but any one of them makes you a shit sheriff," Fargo said. He saw the man's hand start for his gun. "I wouldn't try that," he said. "I don't go around shooting sheriffs, but I could make an exception."

The man's hand fell to his side and he spun on his heel and strode away. Fargo climbed onto the Ovaro, and Penelope came alongside him as he rode slowly on.

"You do speak your mind," she remarked.

"Most times," Fargo agreed as he drew to a halt in front of the Otisville Hotel, a white frame house with a wraparound porch and a fancy white fence in front of it. "You get a room. I'll tend to the horses," he said.

The girl dismounted and hurried into the hotel as Fargo led the horses to a nearby stable. She was waiting when he returned, and he followed her down the hallway to a room on the first floor. She entered and he went to a lone window as she turned on a lamp that lighted a large room with a brass double bed, a dresser against one wall, and two worn stuffed chairs. He peered through the window for a long moment, gauged the distance to the ground at not more than four feet, easy enough to reach from outside. But the window frame was warped, it wouldn't open without creaking. He turned away to see Penelope watching him.

"Where are you staying?" she asked.

"Right here, honey," Fargo said, and saw her lips part at once.

"Absolutely not," she said indignantly. "I'm really grateful to you, but I certainly don't intend showing my gratitude this way."

"What way's that?" Fargo inquired blandly.

"You know what I mean." She frowned angrily.

"Relax, honey." Fargo laughed. "Right now I'm interested in keeping you alive, not satisfied." He saw her eyes narrow as she held back a quick retort. "Somebody tried to get rid of you once. They may try again. I'm staying to make sure they don't do better the second time around."

"You can get a room across the hall or next door. I scream loud," she countered.

"Too far away. Maybe you won't get a chance to scream. I stay here to make sure nobody comes in and you don't go out," he said.

"You don't believe anything I've told you, do you?" she accused.

"Go to the head of the class," he grunted.

"Then why should I believe you? Maybe you don't have any letter. Maybe you're playing your own game of some kind." Penelope frowned.

With an annoyed glance, he pulled the letter from

his pocket and thrust it at her. "Read it for yourself," he said, and she took the piece of paper, unfolded it, and began to read aloud.

"Skye Fargo, General Delivery, Owl Creek, Wyoming. Mr. Fargo . . . I've a special job that will need a special person, the very best, and that means the Trailsman. I promise to pay you one thousand dollars for your services and a five-hundred-dollar bonus when it's done. Enclosed is a hundred dollars for traveling money. The money and this letter will bind my word. Please don't take any other jobs that will keep you from this. Meet me in Otisville, Missouri, in June. I'll be arriving on the weekly stage. P. J. Peabody."

She frowned at him as she handed the letter back. "I don't know anything about this at all," she said.

"Maybe because you're not P. J. Peabody," Fargo said.

"I am, dammit," she flared instantly. "But I don't know what that letter means."

"It means something damn funny is going on. I turned down two good-paying jobs to come here, and I don't aim to be tricked, cheated, or swindled out of the money promised me," Fargo said. "Now I'm going to get some shuteye and I'd suggest you do the same."

"Do I have any choice?" she asked.

"No," he snapped. "Christ, you ought to be pretty done in."

"I am tired," she admitted. "There's a bathroom down the hall. I'll change there," she said, rummaged through her bag, and marched from the room with her things. He went to the door and stayed there as she walked to the bathroom. "You certainly are distrustful." She frowned back at him.

"Wrong word. Try careful," he said, and she sniffed as she closed the door behind her. When she emerged a few minutes later she wore a dark-blue cotton nightdress that reached just below her knees and revealed nicely turned calves. Unlike some women, she had no layers of paint and powder to take off, and so she looked much the same as when she'd gone in to change, except for a freshly scrubbed glow to her face. All in all, he observed again, she had a quiet attractiveness to her, and he could detect no airs that might be expected of a girl playing out a role. But she held her nose in the air as she brushed past him and quickly turned the lamp off inside the room.

Moonlight let in a pale glow through the window and she sat on the edge of the bed as he undressed down to the bottoms of his underwear, aware that she watched the hard-muscled beauty of his powerful physique in the dim light. He stretched out on one half of the bed, and she waited for a few minutes before she pulled the sheet over herself and lay down with it wrapped around her.

"Promise you won't touch me," Fargo murmured.

"Amusing," she said. "You have my word."

"Good night, Penelope," Fargo said. "Or whoever you are."

"Thank you for helping me, Fargo," she said. "For whatever your reasons."

He smiled into the dark of the room. She could hit back. She held herself very still on her side of the bed, he noted as he stretched out. He relaxed and let thoughts wander through his mind. Either she really was Penelope Julia Peabody or she was a damn good little actress. But then most women were born actresses, he mused. Only one fact was clear: somebody didn't want Penelope Julia Peabody alive, a fact that shed absolutely no light on anything else yet, certainly not on the letter that had brought him here. But it was the only place he had to start and he'd have to make the most of it, even if that meant letting her be a target again. She was probably destined to be that, anyway, he reasoned and turned off further thoughts as the sound of her steady, shallow breathing drifted to him. Exhaustion had overcome apprehension, and she slept heavily.

He closed his eyes and let sleep wrap itself around him. But his sleep was that of a wild creature, sleep that hung on the very edge of waking, every subconscious sense alert. But the night passed without interruption, and he woke with the morning sun, swung silently from the bed, and donned trousers. Penelope still slept on her side, and he could see little more than the mass of brown curls against the pillow. He stole from the room, hurried down the hall, and enjoyed the luxury of the bathroom.

When he returned, Penelope was sitting up, sleep still clinging to her face, but she managed a glower as he entered. "Nothing happened. You didn't have to stay here," she muttered.

"Rather be sure than sorry," Fargo said as he finished pulling on clothes. He strapped on his gun belt as she got to her feet. "I'll try to scare up some breakfast while you dress," he said, and left her as she headed down the hall to the bathroom.

The Otisville Hotel boasted a dining parlor opposite the front desk, and Fargo slowed as he neared it to take in the young woman just setting two bags down at the desk. She had eye-catching jet-black hair that hung to her shoulders and that seemed even more brilliantly black against her white shirt.

She glanced up as he neared, and he saw curving, very black eyebrows over black-brown eyes, a short nose, and full, red lips, an attractive, strong face that held just the hint of Mexican blood in the wide, flat cheekbones. The white shirt rested on very round, deep breasts, and a black skirt wrapped around a figure that edged being chunky.

"Registering, miss?" he heard the desk clerk ask.

"Just for the day. I expect someone to come for me," she said, a low, contralto voice. "Penelope Julia Peabody," she said, and Fargo's eyebrows flew skyward as he halted, spun, and stared at the young woman as she finished signing the register.

"Room six," the clerk said, and Fargo saw the frown come over his face as he looked down at the register. "It seems a Penelope Julia Peabody signed in last night. That's strange," he muttered.

"It sure as hell is," Fargo barked, and the girl turned to look at him, black-brown eyes unwavering.

"Are you from the mine?" she asked.

"The name's Fargo . . . Skye Fargo," he said.

Her eyes only stared back. "Is that supposed to mean something to me?" she asked.

"If you're P. J. Peabody it should," Fargo snapped.

"I am Penelope Julia Peabody." She frowned.

"Maybe," he said. "And maybe not."

She drew herself up very straight. It didn't make her much taller, but it pushed the deep breasts tight against the white shirt. "What do you mean by that?" she asked.

"I've a letter from P. J. Peabody, hiring me, signed

and sealed," Fargo said, and saw the surprise come into her face.

"I didn't send you a letter," she said.

"This makes the second time I've heard that. Maybe you're not P. J. Peabody either," Fargo said.

"Either?" she echoed, and the black eyebrows arched.

"This way, honey," he said, and stalked down the hall.

She followed with quick, determined steps that sent the jet hair bouncing back and forth. He yanked the door of Penelope's room open and she turned, dressed, hairbrush in her hand. "Penelope Julia Peabody," Fargo said, "meet Penelope Julia Peabody."

Penelope's brown curls shook as she glanced quickly at Fargo. "What are you talking about?" she asked.

"She says she's Penelope Julia Peabody, here to claim her estate," Fargo said.

"I *am* Penelope Julia Peabody, dammit," the newcomer snapped, black-brown eyes flashing.

"Nonsense," Penelope bit out.

The black-haired girl turned to Fargo. "Is this some sort of bad joke? I'm not amused," she said with a combination of acid and loftiness.

"Me neither, honey," Fargo rasped sharply. "How'd you get here?"

"Paid my way on a wagon train passing this way, people named Anderson. That's easy to check," she said.

Penelope's voice cut in. "If you've come to try to pose as me and steal my inheritance, it won't work.

I've a letter to prove who I am, asking me to come here," she said.

"I've a letter, too," the black-haired girl snapped.

"Wonderful. Everybody's got a letter," Fargo said.

"Only she's a fraud, and so is her letter," Penelope cut in.

"You're the fraud," the black-haired girl threw back.

"One of you is," Fargo put in.

"We'll see about that soon enough. Someone from the Peabody Mining Company is going to pick me up here," the newcomer said.

"To pick me up," Penelope corrected stiffly.

Fargo watched their exchange. They were both sticking to their stories. But they had to, for the moment at least, just as he had no choice but to wait along with them. He decided to interrupt the glaring session. "Guess we'll find out who comes for whom," he said. "Meanwhile, I'm calling one of you Penelope and one of you Penny. You're Penny," he said to the black-haired girl, and started to walk away.

"Where are you going?" Penelope called after him.

"To get some coffee. I'll be near," he said, and strode to the dining parlor, where he got himself a cup of coffee and some bacon.

Penelope closed the door of her room and Penny brought her bags into hers, Fargo saw when he'd stepped from the hotel and crossed the street. He sauntered to where an abandoned supply building let him have a clear view of the front of the hotel, and he settled down behind a corner of the structure. The black-haired Penny's arrival hadn't really added any new questions, he reflected. It had merely made everything take on a new dimension. And someone still had an agreement with him they were going to honor.

He grunted, shifted position, and stayed out of sight as the morning slowly moved toward noon. A few elderly ladies entered the hotel, a young couple, and three delivery men. Noon slid into the afternoon and nothing unusual happened when suddenly he saw the short, energy-filled figure stride from the hotel, jet hair flying behind her. He rose, stepped from behind the structure as Penny hurried down the main street. He stayed back as he followed and watched her halt at the general store. He slid closer as she talked to the storekeeper, and he caught the end of her conversation.

"Yes, I'm at the hotel," she said. "If anyone comes asking for me, please send them there."

"Be obliged to," the storekeeper said, and Fargo stayed back again and watched her move down the street. She planted heels firmly on the ground when she walked and it gave her a little bounce that kept the jet hair swaying. Her deep breasts continued to fill the white shirt, all fullness from the sides as well as the front. She halted at the barbershop, spoke to the barber, and went on until she paused in front of the saloon. Fargo watched her straighten up, draw in a deep breath, and plunge in through the double doors. He hurried, halted outside the doors, and peered over the curved tops. He could see the girl in the center of the floor, the saloon full of drifters, drinkers, card-players, and barflies focused on her.

"Is there anyone here from the Peabody mine?" she called out, and received only silent, curious stares. "I'm Penelope Julia Peabody. If anyone comes looking for me, I'm at the hotel. Thank you very much," she finished, spun on her heel, and Fargo sprang away from the doors to duck behind a pyramid of water casks.

He stayed out of sight as she left the saloon and walked on, stopped again at a hog pen where a half-dozen men were gathered. Too far away to hear, he could tell by her hand movements and her expression that she was saying much the same thing she had inside the saloon. He stayed ducked down behind the casks as she finished, turned, and began to walk back down the main street. He saw the saloon doors swing open and the figure step out, halt, the man's eyes fasten on the girl as she neared. Fargo took in the man, a figure of medium height, black hair under a tan stetson framing a sharp, weasellike face with quick, darting eyes.

He watched the man step forward as Penny drew abreast of the saloon. "You the gal waiting for somebody from the Peabody mine?" the man asked, and licked his lips nervously.

"Yes. Are you from the mine?" Penny asked.

The man's sharp, weasel face glanced quickly around. "No, not exactly, but I know they had some trouble there," he said to the girl. "They maybe can't send anyone for days. I could take you there."

"Oh, that'd be perfect," Penny said, and allowed a quick smile.

"We can take my horse," the man said as he untethered a knobby mare from the hitching post. Fargo saw him cast another quick, nervous glance up the street, and it was plain that he wanted to be on his way.

"No. My horse is at the stable. I'll get him," Penny

said, and Fargo saw the man swallow displeasure as he followed the girl down the street to the stable.

Fargo stayed against the buildings as he followed, darting from doorway to doorway. The man had no connection with the dry-gulchers who had taken Penelope from the stage, Fargo wagered silently with himself. His nervousness all but proved that. He was anxious to get the girl out of town before anyone arrived to interfere with his plans.

Penny reached the stable, hurried inside, and Fargo shrank into a doorway as the man waited outside on his horse, licked his lips again nervously. Penny appeared on a dark-brown gelding and the weasel-faced man hurriedly rode off with her.

Fargo let them pass, darted from the doorway, and raced into the stable, where he flung his saddle on the Ovaro, tossed the stableboy a coin, and rode out into the crowded main street. He paused for a moment in front of the hotel. Penelope would stay in place, he decided. Yesterday's brush with death would keep her from going out to risk another attempt on her life. He spurred the Ovaro forward, skirting his way around the wagons that crowded the street until he caught sight of Penny as she rode from town beside the man.

Fargo slowed, keeping well back to give the girl and her new friend plenty of headway. He turned from the road and climbed up a low slope that let him see the two riders below, still remaining out of sight.

The sharp-faced man turned after a half-mile and led the way up into the low hills. Fargo followed. The trail moved into rocky terrain, and Fargo slowed as he let the Ovaro pick his way through suddenly rough ground. Below, Fargo saw the man halt, gesture to a narrow defile that went through a tall cropping of rock that suddenly appeared.

The girl listened to him and Fargo saw the man gesture again to the defile. Penny followed as he moved his horse forward. He had obviously convinced her he was taking a shortcut, Fargo grunted silently, and he let the two riders disappear into the narrow defile before he moved down. The passage was barely wide enough for two horses to go through side by side, he saw as he reached its mouth. He entered and moved between the high rock walls at a slow walk. The defile followed a crooked path that finally opened onto a small ravine of craggy rocks and twisted trees where every few feet brought a rock-rimmed hollow. He moved forward carefully until the sound came from almost directly ahead, the girl's voice in a sharp cry of half-pain and half-anger, and he swung from the saddle at once.

He moved forward on foot, clambered over a handful of rocks into still another hollow, moved on to crawl up another line of rocks. He halted as he came into sight of the two figures. The girl was on the ground, her wrists tied, and the weasel-faced man was binding her ankles with a length of lariat.

"Who are you? Why are you doing this?" he heard Penny ask.

"You're gonna make me a big payday, girlie," the man said, a whine of gleeful anticipation in his voice. "I might just hold an auction for you."

Fargo drew the big Colt as he edged forward, climbed over the rocks with the silence of a lynx on padded paws. He leveled the revolver as he spoke softly. "Stay right there," he said, and saw the man stiffen instantly. Slowly, the man turned his sharp, weasel face until he could see the big man with the big Colt only a few feet from him. He stayed frozen in space, aware that a bullet would tear into him before he could turn, spin, or dive aside. "Get up, nice and slow," Fargo said as he took another step forward.

But the man had more than a weasel's face, Fargo learned. He had the weasel's quick cunning as he started to push himself upward but suddenly flung himself down atop the girl, locked arms around her as he clung to her. "Go on, shoot," he muttered, and Fargo's lips pulled back as he cursed silently. The weasel-faced varmint knew exactly what would happen if Fargo fired the Colt. At that range the bullet would go right through him and into the girl. "I don't see you shootin', mister," the man said, and suddenly rolled onto his back, his arms around Penny, and she became an instant shield covering him almost completely. "You shoot and you got to hit her," the man rasped. "Now you just back off, cousin."

"No dice," Fargo said. "Let her go."

"Shit I will. Back off," the man said, confidence coming into his voice, and Fargo saw his right hand start to slide down toward his gun as he kept his arm beneath Penny. Fargo felt his finger quiver against the trigger, but he held back. There was no chance for a clean shot, and the man's hand continued to slide toward his holster almost completely hidden by Penny's body. Fargo backed, almost ran, unwilling to hand the man another advantage, and vaulted behind the first line of rocks to disappear from sight.

"Get back here where I can see you," he heard the man shout. But Fargo stayed silent, crouched behind the rocks. "You hear me?" the man called, and Fargo caught the nervousness in his voice.

"Dammit," the man muttered, and Fargo heard him scramble to his feet and pull Penny up with him. Fargo remained absolutely silent and the voice shouted again. "Goddamn, I'll kill her," the man threatened. Fargo stayed silent; the threat was hollow. Penny was only good to him alive. "I'll blow her damn head off," the shout reverberated sharply, and the echo was its only answer.

The man was a nervous, small-time gunhand to begin with. Silence would only unnerve him more, Fargo knew. He heard the man moving behind the rocks, pulling Penny along with him. Fargo backed across the little hollow on silent, catlike steps and lowered himself behind a row of jagged-edged boulders. His eyes were peering hard at the little hollow as the man came into view, pushing Penny in front of him, his gun in one hand. "Son of a bitch," the man snarled. "I'll kill her, I swear it."

Fargo continued to keep silent and saw the man sweep the hollow of land with a flashing, nervous glance. He stayed behind Penny, but standing and moving, she was no longer the complete shield she had been on the ground.

"You comin' out, goddamn ya?" the man shouted. "I'll blast her."

"He's gone," Penny said. "He'll be coming back with help."

"Shutup," the man shouted, and there was fear and uncertainty in his voice now.

Fargo peered through a crack in the rock, the big Colt aimed, and watched the man drag the girl sideways. He followed the two figures with the six-gun. The man pushed her forward, and she stumbled, half-fell. He started to yank her up at once. But he was in the clear for a brief instant, and Fargo's finger tightened on the trigger. The shot sounded as though it were from a small cannon in the rocky hollow, and the weasel face seemed to fly apart in sharp shards of bone and splattering tissue. The figure flew backward and Penny dropped facedown with a sharp cry and lay there as Fargo vaulted over the top of the rocks and strode to her.

He reached down and pulled her to her feet. She stared for a moment at him, black-brown eyes wide, and then came against him with an embrace of relief. He could feel the warmth of the soft, deep breasts through his shirt as she clung to him.

"Oh, my God," she murmured, and finally pushed back, the deep eyes peering up at him. "How did you find me here?" she asked.

"Followed you from town," Fargo said, and the black eyebrows arched in surprise. "Get your horse. We'll talk on the way back," he said.

She drew a deep breath that tested the fabric of the shirt again, retrieved her horse, and followed him as he led the way back through the narrow defile.

"What was that all about?" she asked when they emerged on the other side and she came up beside him.

"Wanted to ask that varmint more about that, but it didn't work out," Fargo said. "I've some ideas, but this sets me to wondering more."

"Well, I don't understand any of it," she said, and her frown seemed as real as the other Penelope's had been. "But I do thank you. I'm really indebted to you, Fargo. Lord knows what would've happened if you hadn't been there."

"Nothing good, you can be damn sure of that," he said.

"I'm sure of that," she said gravely. "If you stay around, I'm sure I can thank you in a more material way. I really don't know what I might be inheriting, though the word 'fortune' was used."

"Oh, I'm staying around for a spell at least. Till I get the money promised me for coming," Fargo said. "Tell me about that letter that brought you here."

"It said I could inherit the Peabody fortune if I came in person to claim it," she told him.

"It was from your father," Fargo said, and she nodded. "And it came as a complete surprise. You never knew anything about him," he went on.

"That's right," she said, frowning back. "My ma never mentioned him. So far as I knew, he was dead, a part of her past."

"Your ma raised you alone," Fargo said, and drew another frown of surprise.

"Yes, mostly in Texas. She was half-Mexican. She ran a little trinket store and I helped her when I grew old enough."

Fargo lapsed into silence as thoughts tumbled through his mind. Her story was an echo of the one the other Penelope Julia Peabody had given him, a little fact that didn't help to clarify a damn thing. If one was the truth, the other had to be a careful and clever fabrication, he pondered. But there was something more in the picture. The real and the fake Penelope had one thing in common: somebody didn't want either one of them around.

"I suppose all I can do now is wait some more," the girl said, cutting into his thoughts. "Someone should come to pick me up."

"Wait and stay the hell out of sight. Announcing yourself all over town was pretty damn dumb," Fargo said. "But then, you didn't know about yesterday."

Her frown was instant. "What about yesterday?" she questioned as they reached the edge of town.

"A passel of dry-gulchers dragged Penelope off the stage. They had orders to kill her. I happened to change their plans," Fargo said.

The girl stared at him with shock that he saw turn to fury. "That bitch," she bit out. "That rotten little bitch. That explains it."

"Explains what?" Fargo questioned.

"She told me nobody would come for me because they didn't know I was around," Penny said.

"Penelope said that?" Fargo frowned.

"That's right, little Miss Brown Curls. It made sense. I couldn't give an exact date when I'd be arriving. I'd just written sometime in mid-June. I told her I'd see to it that people knew that the real Penelope Julia Peabody had arrived."

"What'd she say?"

"She said that was a good idea," Penny said, and Fargo laughed. "Now I understand. She sent me out to be taken in her place, the little bitch."

"So little Penelope put the idea into your head," Fargo said, and couldn't help the smile that stayed on his lips. "I'll be dammed," he murmured.

"She's not going to get away with that," the black-haired girl hissed as they drew up in front of the hotel. She swung from the saddle and strode into the hotel as Fargo followed, reached her as she pounded on the door of Penelope's room. The door opened and Penelope stepped out.

"*Bitch*," Penny spit at her, and followed with a

*41*

resounding slap across the face. Penelope recoiled from the blow, her cheek growing red instantly. "You sent me out to get killed," the black-haired girl shouted, and swung again.

But Penelope twisted away, drove a quick, short blow with her fist doubled that landed in the other girl's ribs and drew a grunt of pain. She followed with a leap that landed her on Penny, and the girl staggered, stumbled, and went down with Penelope half atop her. Fargo saw Penny's black hair bounce as she rolled, came up clawing and hitting with both hands in an explosion of fury as both girls rolled on the floor to an accompaniment of screams and curses. He saw Penelope fasten onto a handful of jet locks and pull as Penny drove a knee into her stomach and both let go, rolled away, and started to dive at each other again.

Fargo's big form stepped between them, his arms wrapping around each as he spun both into the wall with enough force to make their heads bounce. "That's all for that," he growled, kept one hand on each, and waited until both drew a long breath. He released his grip and stepped back. "Go into your room and stay there," he said to Penny. She glowered at him but obeyed, slammed the door shut after her. "Inside," he said to Penelope, and followed her into her room, where she quickly straightened her blouse, which had come open. "You can't blame her for being mad," Fargo said. "You surprise me, honey. That wasn't very nice."

"I wanted to see if they'd try again," she said with almost an airiness.

"So you sent her out as a target," Fargo said chidingly.

"Not really," Penelope answered, a Cheshire-cat

smugness coming into her face. "I knew you'd be out-side watching."

"What if I wasn't?" he pushed at her.

"But you were. I was right. That's all that counts," Penelope snapped with an edge of triumph. "She was so mad I assume they made a try for her."

"Not the ones who went after you. A varmint with ideas of his own," Fargo said.

"And you saved her neck?" Penelope said, a trace of bitchiness in her tone.

"The way I did yours," Fargo said.

She paused for a moment. "Yes," she said finally, a flatness in her voice, admission and something more.

"Be back in a few minutes," Fargo said as he left her and crossed the hall. Penelope was turning out to be a lot more than nicely medium, he decided as he knocked on the door.

Penny opened, her black-brown eyes still smol-dering as she let him in. "You comfort her?" she snapped waspishly.

"I didn't stay to comfort her, and I didn't come to comfort you," he returned, and silently marveled at the complexities of females. "But she didn't just toss you to the wolves."

"You could fool me," Penny sniffed.

"She figured I'd be outside watching," Fargo said.

"How thoughtful of her," Penny said.

"I'm not making excuses for her," Fargo said. "But she did count on my being there."

"I'm so grateful," Penny said with acid.

"Good, because we're all sleeping together tonight. Won't that be cozy?" Fargo smiled.

"You're out of your mind. I've my own room." She frowned.

"I can't watch two rooms at once. Somebody might come trying again tonight. You want to stay alive?" he barked. "Get your things now." He walked to the door, yanked it open, and waited.

She frowned in protest, but she took her bags and followed him to Penelope's room, her deep, round breasts bouncing as she walked on angry, crisp steps.

He went into the room and she came after him and he let the two young women glare at each other for a long moment. "That'll do," he said, and drew a cool stare from Penelope.

"What's this all about?" she asked.

"It's about you sleeping together here where I can watch you," Fargo said, and saw only a mild displeasure in Penelope's eyes.

"I expected you'd want something like this," she said.

"Good," he said. "Something's going on here that gets stranger and stranger. You two keep on playing whatever game you're into, but I'm going to get at the truth."

"I'm not playing any game," Penelope said crossly.

"I certainly am not," Penny said quickly.

"Whatever you say, girls," Fargo grunted. "Meanwhile, I'm going to get you some dinner. I want you to stay well. You're both important to me."

"As human beings or as bait?" Penny tossed back.

"Both," Fargo said as he strode from the room.

He stopped at the dining parlor, ordered the meals, and continued out into the street, where dusk had begun to settle. He peered up the street, saw the narrow, long body in front of the office, strolled forward, and let the sheriff see him. The man came toward him at once. Fargo halted.

"You know anything about a gal going around town saying she's the Peabody gal?" the sheriff asked.

"News gets around," Fargo said.

"She's not the one you brought in last night from what I hear," Sheriff Hazer said.

"You heard right, she's not," Fargo said.

"You mean there are two of them?" The sheriff frowned.

"Seems that way," Fargo said. "Why so interested suddenly?"

"Don't get smart again, Fargo. It's my job to keep on top of things," the sheriff growled.

"Yes, I noticed," Fargo returned. The man's lips tightened, but he held back a reply. "I've got both of them now," Fargo said. "Anybody wants to get at them has to get rid of me first. Any more questions, I'll be at the saloon later. I need a drink."

"No more questions from me," Sheriff Hazer said, and Fargo strolled back to the hotel.

Fargo had gotten an answer and planted a seed. News of Penny's arrival had spread. Maybe the sheriff would spread it even more. Or maybe not. Sheriff Hazer was still a large question mark, either a man bursting with precaution, or a man bought and paid for.

He put thoughts of the sheriff aside and returned to the hotel. He picked up the meals and carried them into Penelope's room. Both girls ate hungrily as they sat in opposite corners of the room. Fargo perched atop the double bed as he ate and stretched out when he finished. Letting the meal digest, he ignored the tension that hung in the air.

When he'd rested enough, he sat up, took in both

girls with a firm glance. "I'll be gone for a spell," he said. "You don't go out and you don't answer the door except for me. That's an order, and it goes for both of you."

Penelope nodded, and her glance held an edge of concern. "Where are you going?" she asked.

"To the saloon. I already let it be known I'd be there," he said.

"Isn't that asking for trouble?" Penelope said.

Fargo shrugged. "You want to see what's at the bottom of a kettle, you stir it up."

"Sounds foolish." Penny sniffed.

"There'll be no surprises. I'll be on guard," Fargo said as he walked to the door. "Remember this, somebody doesn't care which of you is for real and which isn't. You both stay here."

They nodded, each with a half-grimace of displeasure as he closed the door behind him. They'd stay in the room, he was reasonably sure. Both had .tasted enough of fear to take his advice, and he hurried through the night street toward the saloon. There'd be no surprises, he'd told both girls, but he was wrong, he realized when he reached the doors of the saloon. Two men wearing sheriff deputy badges halted him as he entered.

"Got to check your gun, mister," the one said. "Sheriff Hazer's orders." He gestured to the six-guns piled onto a table just inside the doors.

"What's the idea?" Fargo asked.

"The sheriff wants to stop folks from killin' each other in gunfights brought on by too much whiskey," the deputy said.

"Sounds reasonable," Fargo said, and handed the Colt to the deputy and watched the man place it on the table. Fargo walked into the bar as his thoughts pushed at one another. The deputy's answer had been smooth and quick, but it didn't set right. There was more. Sheriff Hazer hadn't been concerned for the life of a girl dragged from the stage. His concern over saloon gunfights didn't fit.

"Bourbon," he said to the bartender, and the man poured the amber liquid. "Sheriff's orders affect business?" he asked mildly.

"Can't say yet. First time he's done it," the bartender said.

Fargo kept the grim smile inside himself. A sudden ruling—no concern for life in it, no coincidence, either. He'd wait for the final piece to show itself. It wasn't much of a wait as he had taken only another draw of the bourbon when the little figure entered the saloon, the half-hopping, half-limping gait unmistakable. Close behind him, something resembling a walking oak tree lumbered in. Fargo took in the figure, at least six feet six inches tall, he guessed, shaggy, dark hair that hung in long, thick strands from a face that seemed made out of bark, lined with deep ridges in dark, almost brown skin. Hollowed eye sockets held wild, staring eyes, and his arms were long as branches, hands made for holding sledgehammers. Fargo knew the type, all raw power, pure muscle, sinew and bone.

Fargo saw the little man's eyes scan the saloon and fasten on him, and then he nodded toward his companion. Fargo's gaze went back to the tall figure, his eyes narrowing as he watched the man head toward him. He spotted one thing in his appraisal: the giant, for all his size, had a thin neck with none of the thick folds at the back of it that provided shock absorption.

He finished his bourbon as the giant reached him, the little man half-hopping, half-limping behind him.

"You're the varmint that stole my horse," the oak tree roared.

Fargo's smile held an edge of sadness in it. The final piece had come to bring it all into place. The good sheriff's no-guns order was clear now, Fargo murmured silently. His Colt would have more than equalized the odds. Now he could be beaten to death, and it would all be but another barroom brawl.

"Did you hear me, mister?" the giant barked.

"I heard you. You've got the wrong man," Fargo said calmly.

"You calling me a liar?" the oak tree thundered.

Fargo smiled. The giant had orders to start a fight with him. Any excuse would do. There was no reason to put off the inevitable. This would be survival, not sportsmanship.

"I'm calling you an ugly, stupid, lying bastard," Fargo said almost pleasantly.

The tree's face flooded with surprise first, then rage, and the towering form leapt forward, both arms outstretched. Fargo held his position, gauged split seconds. The giant's hands were almost at him as the man lunged with all his power when Fargo twisted, dropped halfway down, and spun aside. He heard the man's grunt of pain as the tall figure's midsection slammed full force into the edge of the bar.

Fargo brought a long, looping left up and smashed it into the small of the man's back, and the tall figure slid down onto one knee with another grunt of pain. Fargo stepped in to follow up his success, the blow one that would have broken most men in two. He drew his right arm back to smash it down onto the man's neck when one long leg kicked out backward, all the suddenness and force of a mule's kick in the blow. Fargo tried to twist aside, but he'd been too bold and the blow caught him on the top of his thigh.

He felt the explosion of pain run down his leg as he fell sideways and saw the tall form pull himself to his feet. The giant charged again, and Fargo tried to rise, but his leg was numb. He let himself fall again as the tree threw a sweeping right that just grazed his head. Fargo felt the numbness still in his leg and he rolled under one of the round tables with a top of thick wood. He hit the legs, yanked at them, and brought the table down in front of him as a shield. The lunging figure slammed into it, and his head and shoulders came down over the edge. From the floor, Fargo swung an uppercut that hit the man's jaw, and the head disappeared back behind the tabletop. The blow had only a moderate amount of power behind it, but it bought Fargo a few seconds more of time. As the numbness began to fade in his leg, Fargo pulled himself to his feet, and his leg held as he came around the overturned table.

The tall figure moved toward him, a shade more carefully now, long arms outstretched, the wild eyes looking for an opening. Fargo let his left drop a fraction and the tree lashed out with surprising speed, and Fargo had to duck back to avoid the long-armed blow. But the man came in with a flurry of long, straight-armed blows, lefts and rights thrown in clusters. Fargo found himself hard-pressed to parry, duck away, spin, and deflect the attack. He tried to come in under one looping left and succeeded only in grazing the side of the barklike face. The tall figure weaved as it came in again, and Fargo tried to set himself for an accurate and hard right but had to duck away again as the man unleashed two long, sweeping blows.

Fargo half-circled, crouched, recognizing the man's long arms were the first problem, his sweeping blows and straight-armed punches polelike in their length. Fargo stayed low, stepped in, and tried a looping left that was too short; then he moved in instantly with a hard right that landed in the man's stomach. The tall figure grunted as he bent half over, and Fargo stepped in with a hard left cross aimed at the same spot. The man got one arm up in time to block it, shot out one long leg, and Fargo felt the foot hook in behind his calf. His leg pulled out from under him, and he went down hard. He had time only to see the kick coming at him as he tried to twist his head away, but the boot caught him alongside the top of the temple. He went sprawling half across the floor from the force of it as his head exploded in red and purple flashes.

He felt the huge hands on him as he rose to all fours and tried to shake his head. The man yanked him half up and backward, wrapped one long arm around his neck, and began to squeeze. The pressure somehow made the red and purple flashes disappear, but Fargo felt his breath being shut off almost at once. Forcing a deep breath through his constricted throat, he jammed his elbow backward with all his remaining strength, felt the point of it sink into the man's flat belly. The grip around his throat loosened for an instant, and he swung his shoulders and tore from the man's hands. Fargo threw himself forward and felt one long arm swipe at his neck again and barely miss. He hit the floor, rolled, his breath still coming in harsh, rasping gasps. He spun on one knee, saw the treelike figure charging at him with too much momentum to stop with one blow. He dived sideways, rolled across the floor, and came up with the flat top of the upended table at his back.

The tree had spun again and came at him with another rush. Fargo moved forward and parried half-a-dozen blows the long, sweeping arms hurled at him. The man was too hard-muscled to bring down with body blows, Fargo decided, and the length of his arms made getting in close almost impossible. The man was out to kill him, and he'd almost succeeded once. He was too dangerous to give another chance, and his body of muscle and sinew would take too long to wear down. Fargo eyed the heavy, round tabletop on its side just behind him, the wide, curved edge of it up into the air, and he half-circled, avoided two more polelike blows, tried a punch that fell short, and ducked away from a kick. He circled again until his back was directly to the upended table. He moved in on his attacker, lashed out with a right and a left he knew would be short, ducked, and tried a left hook the long arms easily blocked. He was on his toes, ready for the answering flurry of blows, and he blocked each as he moved backward.

Suddenly he let himself slip and went down on one knee. He seemed to try to regain his feet, but he let his hands hang low. The man leapt at once, his lips pulling back in a snarling grin as he sensed the opportunity he wanted. He lunged forward with all his strength, then loomed upward. Fargo held for a half-second longer, forcing himself not to move. The huge hands were almost at his neck again, the tall figure rushing at him, when he gathered his muscles and flung himself down onto his hands and knees. The

*51*

hurtling long legs slammed into him, and Fargo saw the tall form catapult over him. The man tried to bring his arms up, but it was too late. His jaw came down on the thick edge of the upended table with all his weight and momentum behind it. Fargo heard the sharp sound of neck vertebrae breaking as the man's head snapped upward and back. He spun, leapt to his feet to see the tall form, the head tilted so far back it seemed about to fall off, slowly slide down against the face of the table that rested on its side.

Fargo yanked the figure back by one leg, ready to bring down a final, finishing blow. But there was no need, he saw, as the man lay facedown, motionless. He looked, appropriately enough, not unlike a fallen tree. Fargo lifted his eyes, swept the figures lined up against the walls, and saw movement at the doorway. He glimpsed the little half-hopping figure that disappeared through the figures in front of the doors. He decided against giving chase. His arms ached and his leg still tingled. He drew a deep breath, straightened, and slowly walked to the doorway of the saloon.

"I'll take my gun," he said to the deputy, who watched him with wide eyes.

"Yes, sir," the man said, and handed him the big Colt.

"That little man with the funny walk that just ducked out of here," Fargo said. "Who is he?"

"Ernie Simpson," the deputy said.

"He must work around here," Fargo said as he dropped the Colt into its holster.

"Works for Gordon MacNiff," the man said.

"Where do I find him?" Fargo asked.

"West of town about three miles, big cattle ranch," the deputy said.

Fargo nodded and walked into the night. He slowly made his way back to the hotel. The night had brought a few answers. He had a name, Gordon MacNiff, and he'd learned that Sheriff Hazer was not merely a reluctant lawman. The sheriff took orders, more than likely from this Gordon MacNiff. Fargo put aside further thoughts as he reached the hotel. He ached, his leg hurt, and he wanted to get a cold compress against his temple, which was throbbing with its own fierceness.

"It's me, Fargo," he said as he knocked on the door of the room and heard the latch unlocked.

Penelope opened, Penny right behind her, and both frowned at the raw red welt on his temple.

"Get me a cold cloth," he said as he sat down on the bed.

Penelope used the cold water from a clay pot atop the dresser to soak a kerchief and he held it to his head as he lay back on the bed.

"No surprises, you said," Penny rebuked.

"I was wrong. But there was none I couldn't handle," he answered.

"Seems you had your hands full doing it," Penelope said.

"A little," Fargo admitted, and pushed himself up while he kept the compress against his temple. "Now I'm going to get some sleep, right here on this bed."

"I'll use my bedroll," Penny said.

Penelope took her things and went to the bathroom, and Fargo waited at the doorway again. He stayed as Penny took her turn. She came back wearing a brown shift that hardly reached to her knees, and he took note of short but nicely curved, firm calves, rounded knees, and the way her deep, very

53

round breasts swayed gently under the loose garment. Maybe in another ten years she'd be a trifle dumpy, he mused, but now her body had the firm energy of youth that gave it a kind of controlled vibrancy.

He finished in the bathroom and the lamp was turned out when he came back to the room. He undressed, felt two pairs of eyes watching him as he stretched out on the bed. He listened to Penny turn in her bedroll and felt Penelope lie down at the edge of the bed.

"Nobody comes for you tomorrow morning, we're going visiting," he growled.

"The Peabody Mining Company?" Penny said.

"Bull's-eye," Fargo said. "I've had enough of games."

"I'm not playing any games," Penelope said, sounding hurt.

"I'm not either," Penny said, sounding offended.

"Somebody is, and it sure as hell isn't me," Fargo said. "Now get some sleep." He closed his eyes, drawing the night around him as he wondered which one of them was pretending.

# 3

He rode easily, unhurriedly, under the noonday sun, Penelope and Penny riding in silence a few paces behind him. The morning had passed, and no one had come for either of them. They'd both been more than willing to go along. Penelope had donned a brown dress that set nicely around her tight, trim figure and echoed her brown curls and brown eyes. Penny had switched to a white cotton blouse with a scoop neck that held an echo of a Mexican peasant's blouse, and her very round, deep breasts pushed smoothly up from the neckline. The girls were very dissimilar except for one thing: they shared a tight-lipped determination.

The depot master had given him directions to the Peabody mine and watched him ride on with the both as a little frown of confusion touched his face. Fargo saw Sheriff Hazer step from his office as they passed, and the sheriff's frown was made more of calculation than confusion. Fargo put the Ovaro into a canter as he hurried out of town. The depot master's directions were clear, and he led the way through land that grew steadily steep with tall hillsides of red, powdery earth covered with hardy scrubbrush, mountain hawthorn, shadbush, and hackberry, all of it plainly good iron-ore land. A path led up into the hills, leveled off, and went straight until it suddenly opened up to a hollow of land bordered on three sides by tall hills. A sign that hung from one nail on a post read: PEABODY MINING COMPANY.

His eyes went to the three hillsides and saw a dozen mine carts on their single tracks, some at the top where mineshaft entrances were clearly visible, others resting closer to the bottom of the hollow. But all had chocks under their wheels, and the mine entrances were boarded closed with crisscrossed planks. Small toolsheds dotted the hollow with a larger supply shed off to one side where a half-dozen wheelbarrows were stacked together. Two wooden water conduits snaked down from the hillsides, both dry, and at the end of the area a large house sat with solid proprietorship.

"It looks shut down," Fargo heard Penelope say, dismay in her voice.

"Tighter'n a pig's bun," he grunted as he rode on. A spiral of smoke came from the chimney of the big house, and he sent the Ovaro forward toward the only sign of life. The rambling house branched off into two wings. It was made of dark wood at the bottom, the top half of white-painted clapboard. As he reined up outside, the front door opened and a woman stepped out to survey the three arrivals. Her sharp, brown eyes flicked from him to the two girls and back again. She peered out of a face he guessed had seen some fifty years go by. She wore her graying hair pulled back in a tight bun, and her mouth was a thin line.

"Mine's closed," she said.

"I noticed," Fargo said blandly, and nodded toward the two girls as he dismounted. "These ladies are here by invitation."

"I'm Penelope Julia Peabody," Penny said.

"I'm Penelope Julia Peabody," Penelope echoed.

Fargo watched the woman look from one to the other and back again as her eyes narrowed. "I don't understand," she said.

"Get in line," Fargo put in.

Her eyes stayed on the two young women. "Somebody sent for you?" she questioned.

"Clarence Peabody. My father," Penelope said. "I've a letter from him."

"I've a letter from him, too," Penny said.

The woman's gaze went from one to the other again. "I don't take to being made fun of," she said.

"No one's doing that," Penelope said quickly.

"Seems there's some confusion, or something," Fargo said. "I figure it'll be straightened out in time. I take it that Clarence Peabody died."

"That's right," the woman said.

"How long ago?" Fargo queried.

"About three months now," the woman said.

"Who are you?" he asked.

"Asa Toomey," the woman said. "I was Clarence Peabody's housekeeper for twenty-five years."

"Then you must know about me," Penelope said.

The woman fastened her with a baleful stare. "I don't know anything about any daughter. I just work here."

57

"He must've said something in twenty-five years."
Penny frowned.

"Clarence Peabody never told me anything except what to clean and what to cook. But then he never told anybody anything much," Asa Toomey said.

Fargo's gaze stayed on the woman. "I don't hear much grief over Clarence Peabody's death in you, Asa," he commented evenly.

Her sharp eyes met his gaze. "Maybe I'm all grieved out," she said.

"Maybe," Fargo allowed, and the woman's expression didn't change. "Anyway, these young ladies have a claim, and they'll be staying to prove it."

"Plenty of room here," the woman said.

"My letter says I should first see Mr. Mike Shaw," Penelope said.

"Mine, too," Penny chimed in.

"*First?*" Fargo cut in, surprise jabbing at him.

Penelope's gaze was coolly composed. "That's right, first," she said. Penny's eyes echoed her gaze as Fargo glanced at her.

"It's time I saw those letters," he growled.

"I'm ordered to show mine only to Mike Shaw, who will take me to a Judge Stover," Penelope said.

"Me, too," Penny added

"You won't be showing them to Mike Shaw," Asa Toomey interjected. "He was murdered, gunned down a few weeks back."

Fargo saw the shock flood both girls' faces and felt his own lips purse in thought as his eyes held on Asa Toomey. "Clarence Peabody's been dead three months, the mine's closed down, and the mine manager was killed a few weeks back," he said. "Why are you still here?"

The woman met his eyes with her face expressionless. "Before he went, Mr. Peabody paid me a year's wages in advance to stay on and keep the house in order. I keep my word," she said.

"Good enough," Fargo said when Penny's voice interrupted.

"That proves he was expecting me," she said.

"Me," Penelope snapped.

Fargo half-shrugged. "Expecting somebody, maybe," he allowed.

"Come with me. I'll take you to the guest rooms," Asa Toomey said to the two girls, and they picked up their bags and followed her down a wide corridor. Fargo stepped into the big living room and found a comfortable place with good, oak furniture and walls hung with mining tools as decoration against fiber mats. It gave the room a very distinctive and personal touch.

The sound of a wagon outside made him turn, and he stepped from the house to see the young woman rein up in a dark-green buckboard. She stepped down from the wagon, wearing a blue dress with white edging that clung to her tall, slender figure. Longish breasts turned up at the bottoms, and her hair had a definite auburn tinge as it hung loose around a very attractive face with an aquiline nose, perfectly formed lips, and widely spaced light-blue eyes. She turned a cool, contained gaze on him.

"Are you Mr. Mike Shaw?" she asked.

"Sorry," he said.

"Could you find him for me? Please tell him Penelope Julia Peabody is here," she said.

Fargo felt his lips drop open as he stared at her. "Goddamn," he murmured.

A tiny furrow touched her smooth, high brow. "Is something the matter?" she asked.

"You could sure as hell say that, honey," Fargo said. "I'm hearing and I'm seeing, and I don't believe either."

"I *am* expected," the young woman said.

"And you've a letter to prove it," Fargo said.

It was her turn to stare back in surprise. "Why, yes," she said, and the tiny furrow deepened in her brow.

"From your father, whom you never knew, never heard anything about before you got the letter, right?" Fargo said.

Her lovely lips parted and she pulled them back together as she swallowed. "How did you know that?" She frowned.

"Tea leaves," he growled. "The name's Fargo, Skye Fargo, and that doesn't mean a damn thing to you, right again?"

"I'm afraid not," she said.

"Join the party, honey, whoever you are," Fargo said.

"I'm Penelope Julia Peabody." She frowned.

"So's everybody else," Fargo snapped, and turned to the house as the door opened and Penelope and Penny came out.

"Guess who's here?" he said to the two girls. "Another Penelope Julia Peabody."

The two girls stared at the new arrival. "She can't be," Penelope said.

"Am I to understand you two claim to be me?" the newcomer said, taking in both girls with a frown of cool, contained disapproval.

"I don't *claim* to be anybody. I am Penelope Julia Peabody," Penelope said.

"Except that I'm Penelope Julia Peabody," Penny said.

The new arrival kept her cool composure, Fargo saw, her light-blue eyes unwavering as she stood her ground beside the buckboard. "This is ridiculous," she said calmly.

"Amen," Fargo agreed.

The tall girl's eyes held something close to contempt, Fargo noted, as she swept both Penny and Penelope with a glance. "Whatever you were trying to do, it's over now. You can pack up and leave and take whatever fake letters you have with you," she said.

"I don't have any fake letter, and I suggest you take your own advice and leave," Penny threw back angrily.

The girl turned to Fargo. "They're lying," she protested.

"I've heard that before," he said.

"Are you with the mine?" she asked him.

"They'll fill you in about me," he said, and nodded toward Penny and Penelope. He glanced at the auburn in her hair again. "You'll be Pepper," he said.

"I have a name," she said firmly.

"You've a new one for now," Fargo said, his glance going to the wagon. "You come all the way in that buckboard?"

"Yes, paid my last dollar for it," the girl said.

"All the way from where?" Fargo questioned.

"Kentucky," she said, and he grunted as he swung onto the pinto.

"Where are you going?" Penelope called.

"Away. This is out of hand," he snapped.

"You'll be back, won't you?" she asked, alarm quick in her voice.

"I don't know," he said. "I'm not one for walking away from a thousand dollars promised me, but I might just do it."

"Please come back," Penelope said.

"Yes, please," Penny echoed.

"Is that care or fear?" he tossed at them.

"Maybe both," Penelope said, and Penny's eyes agreed.

"I should like to know what this is all about," the newcomer said stiffly.

"They'll fill you in," Fargo said, and his eyes went past her to hold on Penelope and Penny again. "If I come back, I'll come to find out which one of you is for real," he warned. "That's going to make two of you unhappy. You still want me to come back?"

"Yes, I've nothing to be afraid of," Penelope said quickly.

"Me neither," Penny snapped.

"I certainly know who I am," Pepper said coolly.

"Goddamn," Fargo muttered as he sent the Ovaro into a fast canter.

He turned up one of the paths that led into the hills and rode along a dry water sluice, his thoughts whirling like the horses of a carousel. He hadn't thrown an idle threat at them. The whole business was growing crazier every day. Three girls, each using the same name, each claiming a letter to prove their right to an inheritance, each with essentially the same damn story. One of two was real, he'd been sure, and now suddenly it was one of three. Or maybe he'd been wrong in the first place. Maybe they were all trying to work a phony claim, he pondered. Fake claims to snare a fortune had been tried before. It wasn't all that unusual. Yet this didn't fit the pattern. Three girls, each peddling the same story and the same claim. Perhaps there had been a mix-up, a master plan that had gone wrong. He was reaching far out, Fargo realized grimly. Questions followed questions. He had been brought out here by a letter of agreement that promised big money. Why? he wondered. To meet three girls who knew nothing about the letter he'd received?

Only two things were clear: somebody had wanted him here, and somebody didn't want Penelope Julia Peabody here alive, not a fake one or a real one. It wasn't a hell of a lot to work from. He needed more background. The letters they claimed proved their right to a fortune would be a start. He'd demand to see them, he mused as he rode. Maybe knowing more about Clarence Peabody might help, Fargo thought as he slowed in front of one of the boarded mine entrances. He let his gaze slowly sweep the mining carts, the pieces of equipment lying about, the wooden chutes that ran zigzag down the hill. His tracker's eyes halted at little things most men would have passed by. Little mounds of earth had collected behind the wheels of the empty carts, pushed there naturally by wind, rain, and gravity. New blades of grass grew up along the edges of the wood chutes. Layers of dirt covered some of the equipment, and rust spots had formed on others.

Asa Toomey had said that Clarence Peabody passed on some three months back. The implication left was that the mine had shut down then. But the mine had closed down a lot before that, closer to a year than three months, Fargo guessed. He frowned at one more thing that didn't fit right. His thoughts continued to circle as he rode higher into the hills. He had crossed over a narrow passage when he saw the thin plume of rock dust rising into the air from behind a crag some hundred yards on. He turned the horse and headed up toward the plume, and as he neared he heard the sound of a pickax on rock and a thin, reedy voice singing.

He skirted the pinto around the crag, aware the horse's hooves were loud on the rocky ground. The singing and the sound of the ax stopped as he reached the other side and reined up. He saw the figure standing, watching him with one hand on the pickax, the other on an old fowling piece. Fargo guessed the man to be in his sixties, at least, a short, almost elfin figure with a gray circle of hair cut in monk's style, sharp blue eyes set in a round face that retained a vibrant vitality despite the leathery skin. A miner's pack rested beside a sturdy-legged dark-brown pony nearby.

" 'Morning. Didn't mean to disturb you," Fargo said cheerfully.

The man's hand drew back from the rifle. "No fuss, stranger. I just try to stay careful. You never know when a stray Pawnee or Osage might come by," he said.

"It's good to be careful," Fargo said, and let his gaze linger on the pickax and the small tool pack. "You can't be mining iron ore with a pickax," he said.

"Just lookin' to find a good deposit. I find one, I'll do the real mining later," the little man said.

"Been working these hills for long?" Fargo asked.

The man's round face wrinkled into a wry laugh.

"I'd say so, young feller. Some fifty years. Made enough to keep me happy, but mining becomes a habit," he said. "Name's Joe Plum."

Fargo nodded as he slid from the Ovaro. "Fargo . . . Skye Fargo," he said.

The round, leathery face peered at him. "The Trailsman?" Joe Plum asked.

"Some call me that," Fargo conceded.

"You broke a new trail for George Willis through Comanche country 'bout five years ago," the little man said.

"That's right." Fargo smiled.

"George is an old friend. He told me all about it, said you were something special. Right glad to meet you, Fargo," Joe Plum said. "What brings you to these parts?"

"Been wondering about that myself," Fargo said ruefully, and he studied the little man for a moment. "If you've been working these hills for fifty years, you must've known Clarence Peabody," he ventured.

"Better than most, though nobody ever knew Clarence real well," Joe Plum said. "Why?"

"Because I've a real strange problem," Fargo said, and felt the excitement stab at him as he regarded the old miner. "And maybe you're just the man that can help me."

"Me?" Joe Plum frowned.

"You could be just who I need. If you've time to listen to the strangest damn story I'll be glad to tell it to you," Fargo said.

Joe Plum put down his pickax and leaned back against a rock. "Son, time's what I have most of. Start tellin'," he said.

Fargo began by showing the little man the letter he

had received, waited till Joe Plum finished reading it. "That's what brought me here. It's what's happened since I got here that has me buffaloed," he said.

He went on quickly, started with his waiting to meet the afternoon stage and everything that had followed since. He left nothing out, detailed each girl's reaction and steady insistence that she was the real Penelope Julia Peabody. He finished with the arrival of the third Penelope, and when he did, Joe Plum rubbed a hand across his leathery face and let his lips purse.

"Well, you sure didn't exaggerate any," the old miner said. "That's one strange kettle of fish."

"I'm thinking the truth might lie as much in yesterday as in tomorrow, and you can open up yesterday for me," Fargo said. "I aim to get the money promised me. I'll pay you two hundred of it if you'll help."

"You've got yourself a deal, Fargo," Joe Plum said. "I can start with a damn good guess why the first girl was dry-gulched."

"I'm listening," Fargo said.

"There's a law here which says that if no proper heirs come to claim a man's land within a year it's up for the taking. There are quite a few folks that'd want their hands on Clarence Peabody's land."

"The mine's been closed down for a year or more, I'd guess," Fargo said.

"Bulls-eye. It ran out of good ore at just about the same time Clarence Peabody ran out of good health," Joe Plum said.

"Then why would anyone kill to get it?" Fargo frowned.

"They figure Clarence has a fortune put away somewhere. They're probably right. He made a hell

66

of a lot when the mine was going well and spent damn little of it. He even bragged about stashing it away. Under the law, if they have the land, anything found on it is theirs."

"One of them is a man named Gordon MacNiff. The dry-gulchers were under his orders. He had somebody try to take me out, too," Fargo said.

"Figures. He and Clarence always hated each other," Joe Plum said.

"Seems the good sheriff takes orders from MacNiff," Fargo said.

"Always has," the little man grunted.

"None of this explains the girls or who brought me here," Fargo remarked.

"I'd guess that'll take a lot more doing," Joe said.

Fargo grimaced. "I'd like to have a look at MacNiff's place. He could be getting ready for another try. By now he knows I've brought the girls to the Peabody house. But I ought to check out the house, too, if there's going to be trouble."

"I know where one can get a close look at MacNiff's spread without being seen. You go back to the house. I'll stop by. Give me a few hours," Joe Plum said.

"Good enough." Fargo nodded as he pulled himself onto the pinto. "One more question. You know Asa Toomey?"

"I do," Joe said. "Strange woman, that one. Always felt she hated Clarence Peabody, yet she worked for him all those years. Sometimes I thought she was waiting for somethin' to happen to him."

"According to her, Clarence Peabody died three months ago," Fargo said.

"Only he didn't just die. He did himself in," Joe Plum said, and Fargo felt his eyebrows lift. "Doc

Elder told him a year ago that his lungs were gone. He hung in until it got too bad. Then one day three months ago he rode to Cameron's Gorge, left his horse there, and jumped off the edge. It was the kind of thing Clarence would do."

"I'll want to hear more about Clarence Peabody later," Fargo said. "Meanwhile, take it careful, old-timer. Watch your neck."

"Been doing it too many years to stop now. See you later." The little man laughed and began to clamber onto the sturdy pony.

Fargo rode on around the crag and began the slow trip down the hills. He took a long path that went around the back of the mine and finally emerged where the only road led straight to the house at the end of the base area. He dismounted in front of the house and strode inside.

Penelope and Penny looked up at him from inside the big living room as he entered. Both were quick to mask the moment of relief that flashed in their eyes.

"I meant what I said before. I'm going to get at the truth. Two of you will be sorry then. Maybe all three of you."

"It won't be me," Penelope said.

"Me neither," Penny quickly added.

"Where's the latest Penelope Julia Peabody?" Fargo asked. "In her room?"

"She went out, said she was going to look over the mine, seeing as how it was hers," Penny answered tartly.

"Damn," Fargo spit out as he whirled. "Poking around old mine shafts is no place for an amateur."

He left the house at a run, halted outside to scan the ground. She'd unhitched the horse from the buckboard and he saw the lone set of hoofprints rise up into the steep hillside at the right side of the house. He took the Ovaro up after the tracks that led past two small entranceways to a larger one at the very top of the steep slope. He saw the horse to one side of the mouth of the shaft, and he swung from the pinto and stepped to the crisscrossed planking that blocked the entrance. He saw where she'd squeezed through an opening between the boards. He couldn't fit his shoulders through, so he tore away one of the planks before ducking into the mine entrance.

Only a half-dozen steps into the mine shaft the dank, pungent odor assailed his nostrils, the smell of mine-shaft air that had hung undisturbed for too long. Tiny, invisible particles of rock dust clung in that air, and suddenly disturbed, they sifted into mouth, nose, and ears with silent, killing suddenness, unnoticed until it was too late.

"Damn-fool girl," he hissed aloud as he followed the footsteps clear in the dust-covered floor of the shaft. He wrapped a kerchief around his mouth as he felt the dryness already beginning to come into his throat. Footprints showed where she had halted alongside one of the side beams of the shaft, but she had gone on again and he followed quickly, breathing in behind the kerchief and blowing air out through his nose.

The light from the entranceway had begun to quickly fade away and the blackness of the abandoned shaft stretched ahead when he spied the crumpled form on the mine floor. He was at her in two long-legged strides and saw that she hadn't collapsed from the dust-laden air alone. A length of shoring timber lay beside her where it had fallen from the ceiling, and a trickle of blood ran from her forehead. She was breathing, but barely, he noted as he lifted her and slung her over his shoulder. He felt the tightness in his own chest as he turned and started back toward the entranceway. He was nearing the mouth of the shaft when he dropped to one knee, held his breath behind the kerchief, and gathered himself again. He half-ran, half-stumbled forward, almost crashing against the boards still across the entranceway. He gulped in the fresh air that drifted into the front of the shaft.

He climbed out with the girl still hanging over his shoulder, lowered her to the ground, and saw the whiteness of her face as air barely seeped through her throat. He cast frantic glances about for a high, flat rock and found none. But he spotted a stack of wide planking that would have to do. He unbuttoned the top of her dress where it held her breasts in tightly, laid her on her stomach over the planks so that her head hung down almost to the ground. He half-straddled her as he used both hands to press down along her back, massaging the flesh and muscles that would act on her lungs. His hands like the handles of a bellows, he pressed slowly down and up, trying to force the dust-laden air from her body. He cursed silently as he worked with slow haste.

She coughed suddenly, a sweet sound despite its hoarse, racking quality, and he heard a rasped intake of breath. He pulled his hands back and let her body take over the process of breathing, and she coughed again, stronger this time, and she began to draw in deep breaths. She tried to lift her head, but he held her down for a few moments more, then pulled her up to a sitting position atop the planks. Her cough was a hard, choking sound now, but there was good air in it and he watched the longish breasts rise and fall, very white, smooth skin where the neckline of the dress hung open. She looked at him, blinked, realization returning to her quickly. He went to the pinto and took his canteen down.

"Little sips," he said as he handed it to her, and she nodded as she drew in quick mouthfuls. Finally she drew a deep, clear breath, and he patted the trickle of blood dry on her forehead. "You're damn lucky, honey," he said. "Another five minutes and you'd have been finished."

"The plank just suddenly fell," she said.

"The plank only started it. The air in there would have finished it," Fargo said as he returned the canteen to the Ovaro. He saw her suddenly realize her dress hung open and she pulled the neck closed at once. "A bone-headed stunt," he grunted.

"No stunt," she protested. "I just wanted to look around."

"Bullshit, honey," Fargo said evenly. "It was a one-up move, a take-charge gesture to put the others on the defensive."

A moment of smugness touched her light-blue eyes, but she quickly cloaked it with protest. "Nonsense. They're obviously not very confident of themselves," she sniffed.

"Maybe they've just more common sense," Fargo said. "Think you can ride yet?"

"Of course," she said, got up quickly, and swayed instantly as he caught her. Her head came against his chest as she clung to him until the moment passed, and he drew in the faint sweet smell of her. Her slenderness held a wiry strength against him. She finally pulled back. "Thank you," she murmured. "For everything. I guess I owe you my life."

"I guess," he agreed. "You're not the first, and you won't be the last."

"I don't take a thing like that lightly," she said. "I'll make it up to you properly when I've inherited my fortune." A tiny furrow touched her forehead as she paused and glanced out at the hills. "If there is a fortune," she murmured.

"Why the sudden doubts?" he asked, faintly surprised. It was the first sign of uncertainty any of them had given.

"This place. It's abandoned," she said.

"Doesn't necessarily mean anything," he said.

"I suppose so," she said, and pulled herself onto her horse.

He watched her for a moment. She didn't hold to the determined posture Penny and Penelope did. She was willing to show misgivings and normal doubts. Maybe that said something, he pondered as he started down the hillside with her.

"Tell me something about yourself," Fargo said.

"There's not much to tell. I'm twenty-five, I lived back in Kentucky with my mother and worked in a dry-goods store till that letter came," she said.

"Didn't your ma have anything to say about the letter?" Fargo slid at her.

"My ma went off with a traveling salesman three years ago," the young woman said. "Haven't heard from her since."

"You've been living alone?" Fargo asked.

"Yes, if you can call Mrs. Reilly's boardinghouse living alone," she said.

Fargo's lips thinned. "Very convenient again," he muttered.

Her glance was instantly sharp. "What's that mean?"

"You've all got such convenient stories to tell. Each of you living alone, each of you almost impossible to check out. Nobody with a ma around to react to the letter. It's all too neat and too much the same. Something's goddamn strange."

Her eyes blazed at him. "You're calling me a liar?" she snapped.

"Maybe," he said.

"I don't see why you bothered to save someone who's a liar," she flung back.

"Moment of weakness," Fargo said blandly.

"Go to hell," she hissed, and sent her horse racing down the hillside. He followed at his own pace, and she was standing outside the door of the house when he reached it. Her slender figure was very straight, a hint of contrition in the light-blue eyes.

"I think I picked the right name for you," he remarked as he dismounted.

"I'm sorry. You just saved my life. I shouldn't have gotten so angry. I guess you've the right to call me whatever you like," she said.

"Nothing personal," he said. "Right now you're all in the same very strange boat to me." He went into the house with her, and Asa Toomey came from the kitchen to confront him.

"You'll be wanting a room, too, I take it," she said.

"For now. Near the front of the house," he said.

"First room down the east wing," the woman said, and turned away, but Fargo caught the narrowed thought in her eyes as she scanned the three young women. Penny's gaze went to Pepper and quickly took in the slightly disheveled state of the auburn-haired girl.

"Trouble?" she asked with a hint of tartness.

"Let's say I was lucky Fargo came along," Pepper answered.

"Join the club," Penelope said wryly, her eyes on the big man. "You find out anything when you took off before?" she asked.

"Found out why you're not wanted around here by some folks," he said, and sat down as he told the three young women of his meeting with Joe Plum and what he had learned. When he finished, all three were silent, their faces wreathed in apprehension.

"That mean there are going to be more attempts at getting to us?" Penelope asked after a moment.

"You can count on it," Fargo said. "Anybody want to bow out?" He let the question hang by itself for a moment as he watched their faces. "A good try is better than a pine box," he added.

"I'm certainly not bowing out," Penelope said.

"Absolutely not," Penny snapped.

"No way," Pepper said firmly.

"There's stubborn and there's stupid," Fargo said.

"It's neither. It's a matter of right," Pepper returned. "I intend to have what's my right to have."

"It won't be easy, honey," Fargo said. "You were all to contact Mike Shaw. They made sure you wouldn't be doing that. They tried to stop you from getting here. They're not going to sit back and quit now."

"Will they ever quit?" Penelope asked.

"Once the real heiress is officially recognized,

74

they're out of business. That means one of you has to prove you're the real one," Fargo answered.

"I understand Mike Shaw was going to handle that," Penny said.

"He's not now," Fargo said.

"Will you?" Penelope asked.

Fargo tried to keep satisfaction from his smile and knew he didn't entirely succeed. "I'll help the real Penelope Julia Peabody. Nobody else," he said. "That means you'd better convince me first. You can start by showing me those letters you have. I want to see each one for myself." He sat back as each girl frowned as she wrestled with her own thoughts. The sound of hoofbeats broke into the moment. He rose, started toward the door as Joe Plum rushed into the house.

"Trouble, real trouble," the little man said to Fargo, taking in the three girls with a quick glance. "MacNiff has hired a collection of saddle tramps to come after you here. He was outside the house with them, and I heard enough before I got out of there. He'll wait till after dark and then come. There must have been fifteen of them. With his boys added, he'll throw at least twenty guns at you."

Fargo's lips pulled back in distaste.

"I can shoot," Penny said. "My ma taught me."

His glance went to Pepper and Penelope. "I've done a little," Penelope said.

"I guess I can pull a trigger," Pepper said.

Fargo saw Asa Toomey appear in the doorway. "There has to be some rifles around here," he said.

"Cabinet in the study. Six guns," the woman said.

"Please get them," Fargo said as he walked to the door with Joe Plum and his gaze swept the hollow and the three hills surrounding it. "They have to

75

come in that way," he said, and gestured to the far end of the area. "It's the only way in. I could hold them off with six good marksmen."

"Which you don't have. There's us two and three girls, and only one knows her way with a rifle. Not enough," Joe Plum said. "They'll lay down a barrage and close in while we're busy ducking lead."

Fargo's eyes continued to sweep the scene outside the house, his mind leap-frogging thoughts as his gaze paused at the empty mining carts that were perched high on the hillsides. "Maybe we can make it enough," he thought aloud. "We'll need luck and some fast preparing."

"Such as?" the little man questioned.

"Dynamite." Fargo bit out the word. "Never saw a mine operation that didn't have dynamite around. If there's some in the supply shed, we might just be in business."

Fargo struck out for the supply shed with Joe Plum almost running to stay close. The inside of the shed was the usual collection of boxes, barrels, and tools, and Fargo took one side of the shed while the little miner explored the other. He had reached the back corner when a steel box offered up the contents he sought.

"Got it," he called out, and Joe Plum pushed aside shovels to reach him as he removed six sticks of dynamite.

"You figure to toss the stuff at them, Fargo?" Joe asked. "They'll scatter after the first one."

"I know. I've better plans for this. We're going to make us some artillery," Fargo said as he led the way from the supply shed. Outside, he pointed to three of the mine carts halfway up the hillside. "Set those carts loose and they'll come right down here where we're standing," he said.

"MacNiff's men will have to pass here to attack the house," Joe Plum said.

"Exactly. We're going to fill these carts with loose rock. These hills are full of it. Two sticks of dynamite in each cart, timed to go off as the carts reach bottom," Fargo said. "Cannonballs of rock flying in all directions. Instant shrapnel."

"By God it might just work," Joe said.

Fargo glimpsed Penny step from the house, the other two young women behind her. "Out here," he called. "It's your necks I'm trying to save. You can work for them, too. Start loading rocks into those three carts, and be fast about it."

"What size rocks?" Penny asked as she started to climb toward the first cart.

"Anything you can carry comfortably," he told her as he strode to the next cart and began to toss loose rocks into it. He cast an eye at the sky and guessed there was another hour till night. Just enough time, he murmured silently.

The estimate was a correct one: they finished loading the carts just as darkness began to slip over the hollow. Placing the dynamite sticks in the center of each cart was the last chore, and he gauged the distance to the bottom of the hill as he cut the fuses down. Descent and burning time had to match or it would all have been for nothing, he knew.

When he finished, he returned to the house with the others and had a few mouthfuls of Asa Toomey's stew. Joe Plum waited in the living room with the girls as the night lowered. "Hand out the rifles, Joe,"

Fargo said. "You'll stay here in the house. Position the girls wherever you think best."

"I'll take care of it. Lights out and heads down," the old miner said. His glance took in the three young women. "I'll give you as much instruction as I can in the next half-hour. You'll start shooting when I do. I don't expect miracles. I do expect you'll do your best, ladies. Losin' is going to be permanent."

Asa Toomey appeared in the doorway, and Fargo turned to her. "I'll be locked in my room," the woman said. "I'm no part of this. I've some years to live out, and I intend to do it."

"Understood," Fargo said, and saw her eyes go to Joe Plum, a tightness coming into her already thin mouth.

"What's your interest in this, Joe?" she asked. "You lining up with the other vultures?"

"I'm just trying to find out what old Clarence wanted and see it done," the little man said. "I think that's only right."

Asa Toomey made a wry sound. "Clarence Peabody made people miserable all his life. Maybe he don't deserve any better," she said, and spun on her heel and stalked away.

Fargo went to the door as Penny began to turn down the lamps. "You listen to Joe. He'll put you in the safest spots. When it starts, keep shooting. Keep their attention on you and the house," he said, pulling the door closed after him.

He broke into a loping run as he headed uphill toward the first of the carts. He reached the cart, dropped to one knee behind it as a half-moon rose to bathe the land below in a pale light. He waited with the silent patience of a red-tailed hawk, his eyes fixed on the land below. The sound of the horses came to him first, and he shifted his gaze to the entrance to the hollow as the riders appeared. They moved slowly, halted as they reached the open land, and dismounted. Joe Plum had guessed right, Fargo grunted. There were at least twenty of them.

He waited, one hand poised atop the edge of the cart, and watched the men begin to move toward the house. They spread out in two lines, one behind the other, as they walked forward. The first shot that split the stillness came from the house, and it missed its target. But it served to focus the full attention of the attackers on the house, and they answered with a quick flurry of shots. The first line of riflemen moved forward under cover of the fusillade, dropped to one knee, and lay down another barrage while the second line moved up. They had been well coached, Fargo grunted grimly, and he rose to his feet. The men were almost in line with him below, and he reached into the first cart, struck the match and lighted the fuse on the dynamite. As soon as it sizzled and caught, he kicked the chocks from beneath the wheels and the cart began to roll down its single track.

He was running instantly, headed for the next cart, where he halted, did the same, and ran for the third one. Once again, he lighted the fuse as he leaned into the rock-filled interior of the cart, pushed himself back, and knocked the chocks away. The cart began to roll instantly and he followed, long legs churning, until halfway down the hill he threw himself flat on the ground. He watched the carts race downhill almost in unison and saw the men below halt and turn at the sound of them. They broke ranks to avoid the plunging carts, but Fargo had expected that and he nodded in satisfaction.

"Getting out of the way won't be enough, you bastards," he muttered aloud, and realized his words held a note of desperate prayer in them. If the plan failed, if it somehow didn't go off as he expected it would, they'd overwhelm the house. There'd be no other way to stop them, and he felt his lips pull back in grim anger.

The explosion blotted out his thoughts as the first cart reached the bottom of the hill and erupted in a flash of yellow fire. The other two carts exploded split seconds later, and the hillsides reverberated with the sound. As he watched, he saw the attackers spin and try to race away. But most took hardly more than a half-dozen steps as the night shattered in a hail of stone cannonballs. The rock missiles arched upward and down, flew from all sides, propelled with devastating force in straight lines and cascaded in a deadly rain from above.

He saw the figures fall, some tossed half into the air, and the violence of it was as shattering as it was brief. In what seemed only seconds, the ground was littered with broken and bleeding bodies and smashed heads. Fargo saw two figures trying to flee, half-stumbling, half-running to one side where they had somehow escaped the hail of death. He brought one down with a quick shot from his Colt while the other disappeared into the darkness. He stayed in place, waited, and scanned the scene below. When nothing else moved, he rose and walked down the hillside to the house. Joe Plum came out as he neared, his leathery face wrinkled into a wide grin. "By God, it worked, even better'n you hoped for," the little man said.

"So it did. Anyone hurt inside?" Fargo asked.

"No, but they're still plenty shook up. Bullets were bouncin' all around them." Joe laughed. "It's plain they're not used to that."

Fargo peered across at the bodies that covered the ground. "Too damn many, but I don't want a sky full of buzzards, come morning. We'll have to do something with them," he said.

"I'll ride to town and fetch Hod Hoskins," Joe said.

"The town undertaker?" Fargo asked, and Joe nodded. "Will he come out here now?"

"Hell, the town pays him fifty cents a buryin'. Hod will be tickled as a pig in mud to come out. He'll bring his big stake-side dray and cart 'em all back at once," Joe said.

"Get him," Fargo agreed.

"Be back in an hour or so," Joe said as Fargo started for the house. Lamps went on as he strode into the living room. He took in the three young women, tension still clinging to their young faces.

"It's over, for now," he said. "Sit down and pull yourselves together." Asa Toomey appeared in the doorway, her face expressionless. "Any whiskey around here?" Fargo asked her.

"Cabinet against the wall," the woman said, and hurried away.

He went to the cabinet and found glasses and a half-dozen bottles, Kentucky rye and bourbon, and he poured a shotglass full for each girl. They sipped the whiskey, and color slowly returned to their faces. They met the hardness in his lake-blue eyes as he fastened a long glance on each.

"It seems we owe you again," Penelope said.

"You could be more unhappy than grateful," Fargo said harshly. "It's time for truth. No more fancy talk. No more excuses. No more games. I want to see those letters, each damn one of them." Their faces grew tight at once, but his eyes continued to rake each. "I'll be in my room. You can decide who goes first, but I wouldn't wait too long."

He drained his drink and strode from the room, leaving their silence behind.

# 4

Fargo stretched muscles as he lay on his back across the bed and wondered who'd appear first. It didn't much matter. What mattered was getting a look at those letters they each claimed as proof of their right to be here. The soft knock at the door broke off his musings and he sat up.

The door opened and Penny entered, wide, flat cheekbones seeming flatter than they were by the tightness in her face. She held the square of note-paper tight against her deep, round breasts, a protective stance, and he saw a grimness touch her face as she handed it to him.

"This ought to satisfy you," she murmured as she perched herself on the edge of a chair.

Fargo unfolded the letter, took in the almost straight up-and-down, firm handwriting, and began to read slowly, carefully, weighing each word.

Dear Penelope,
    I realize this will come as a complete surprise to you, perhaps even as a shock. After all, you have

never heard from your father until now. Yes, you are my daughter, and as such, you shall inherit all my worldly goods and possessions.

I have hidden away a small fortune over the years to use in my old age. For all these years I have seen to it that this fortune did not fall into greedy, grasping hands. Even if they had killed me for it, they wouldn't have found it.

But as the doctor has informed me that I will have no old age, I shall have no use for the fortune I have put away. Yet I will not let it fall into the hands of those who have sought after it for so long.

Though this is the first time you have ever heard from me, you are my daughter and you bear my name. As such, all I have is rightfully yours. But you must come here in person and claim it. Bring this letter with you and give it to Mr. Mike Shaw, the foreman of my mine, and he will take you to Judge Stoner. Do not give or show this to anyone else.

I will not tell you any more should this letter fall into the wrong hands. Nor will I tell you why you have never heard from me before now. I have lived my life in my way and I make no apologies to anyone.

Just come and find what is yours. You will not be sorry.

Your father,
Clarence Peabody
Peabody Mining Co.
Otisville, Missouri

Fargo frowned as he handed the letter back to Penny. "Convinced?" she asked.

"Sorry," he said, drawing an instant frown.

"What's wrong with that? What more do you want?" Penny said, black eyes flashing.

"Proof," he snapped. "That letter's long on sentiment and short on details. It doesn't give dates, places, facts. It doesn't furnish any real proof about you. Hell, anybody could've written that letter."

She waved the letter at him. "He admits he's never written before, that this will be a shock and a surprise. Doesn't that mean anything, dammit?"

"Not enough, honey," Fargo grunted.

"I don't care if it's enough for you. I know who I am and that's Penelope Julia Peabody," she flung at him.

His eyes narrowed as he gazed at her. "What'd your mother call herself?" he questioned.

"Maria Montez Peabody," Penny shot back.

"How old are you?" he asked.

"Twenty-three," she said. "And that letter is my proof, whether you like it or not."

"That letter doesn't answer a damn thing," he said.

"I don't care what you think," Penny said as she stormed out of the room.

Fargo sat down on the edge of the bed. He let the letter rewind itself in his mind. Words and no meaningful proof, he grunted. Just like her story, impossible to pin down, full of convenient gaps. All their stories were the same, and he wondered if all their letters would be as vague as Penny's had been. He glanced up as Penelope entered, quiet determination in her face as she handed the letter to him.

He began to read it at once, and the surprise that stabbed at him at the first sentence turned to almost disbelief by the end of the first paragraph. The letter was identical to the one Penny had shown him, not a word different, not a sentence changed. The frown dug deep into his brow by the time he finished.

"What is it?" Penelope asked as he looked up at her.

"Dammed if I know," he said.

"What do you mean? That proves I'm the real Penelope Julia Peabody." She frowned.

"This letter wouldn't prove that, and it proves shit now," Fargo said, and felt anger stab at him.

"Are you saying her letter convinced you?" Penelope asked angrily.

He was about to answer but held back the words that came to his lips. It was plain that Penelope had no idea Penny's letter was identical to hers. He didn't know just what that meant yet, but it had to mean something. He decided to hold back accusations.

"Well? Was her letter so much better than mine?" Penelope pushed at him.

"No, hers didn't convince me either," Fargo said evenly.

"Well, that's just too bad then," Penelope said, and managed to sound hurt as well as angry, a technique she had mastered well.

"How old are you?" he asked.

"Twenty-one," she said.

"What name did your mother use?" he pressed.

"Rose Peabody," Penelope said. "What's that got to do with anything?"

"I don't know. Just asking," he said, the answer honest enough. He handed the letter back and she snatched it from his hand.

"Is that all you're going to say?" Penelope snapped.

"For now," he answered, and she spun on her heel and swept from the room. Fargo still frowned at the half-closed door as it pushed open again and the slender, coldly contained form entered, a half-smile touching her lips with a hint of smugness.

"They're certainly angry. I presume you realized their letters were fakes," Pepper said.

"Maybe," Fargo said, held his hand out, and she gave the letter to him. He unfolded it, read quickly, no surprise stabbing at him this time, only a continuation of monumental disbelief. It was the same as the other two letters, identical in every word, the firm, upright script unmistakably the same. He finished reading it and handed it back to the young woman.

"Join the crowd," he said, and saw the light-blue eyes widen in surprise.

"You can't be serious," Pepper said.

"Guess again," Fargo said.

"That's ridiculous. You can't put my letter in the same boat with whatever fake ones they gave you," she protested angrily. The fury was real, he was convinced as her eyes shot pale-blue fire at him. She, too, had no idea that her letter was the same as the others and again he held back words. "Dammit, you've got to believe one of us, Fargo," she thrust at him.

"I'm going to think some more on it," he said evenly.

"Well, if you can't tell a real letter when you see one, then you'll have problems," she snapped as she walked haughtily from the room.

Fargo drew a deep breath, astonishment still clinging to him as though it were an unwanted cloak. The damned letters had added only a new and stranger twist to the puzzle.

The sound of a wagon outside brought him to the window and he saw two men halting the big stake-sided dray while Joe Plum dismounted in front of the house.

Fargo strode from the room, hurried down the corridor, and crossed the living room.

Penny rose from the settee, the other two girls already in their rooms for the night, and she tossed him a chiding glower. "I'm very disappointed in you," she muttered. "I expected you'd be quicker to tell the real from the fake."

"I'm always disappointing people," he said as he went outside. He beckoned to Joe Plum and led the way to the side of the house.

"You look like you've seen a three-headed frog," the old miner commented.

"Just about," Fargo said, and quickly told Joe about the letters. When he finished, Joe Plum's face had found new wrinkles.

"Damnedest twist," the old miner said. "What do you think it means?"

"I don't know. It's sure as hell thrown me a curve," Fargo said.

"It could mean there's no real one. They could all be fakes," Joe said.

"I thought about that. But why the same letter? That just makes no damn sense," Fargo answered.

"Unless they're being used," Joe said. "Sent here to play out the role. Only maybe something went haywire, got fouled up along the way."

"But they don't know that, so they're each carrying through as they were told to do," Fargo supplied.

"That's right." Joe nodded.

Fargo frowned. The explanation made sense out of something that defied sense. Yet he harbored another thought that refused to go away. "This Doc Elkins that gave Clarence Peabody only a short time to live, I'd like to see him," he said.

"That'll be easy enough. He's in town," Joe said.

"Good, but there's something else I want first," Fargo said, and Joe Plum's eyes questioned. "Gordon MacNiff. It's time he had some of his own medicine," Fargo said, and hardness came into his voice.

"He always comes into town for supplies on Thursdays. That's tomorrow," Joe said.

"You can point him out to me," Fargo said.

"Wouldn't miss it. See you, come morning," the little man said, and Fargo went into the house, now dark and quiet.

He went to his room and undressed to the sound of the big wagon rolling away with its grisly cargo. He stretched out on the bed atop the sheet in the warm night, and moonlight seeped in through the window to bathe the power of his naked body in a pale silver light. He let his thoughts wander of themselves. Nothing made any sense, not even as a fast swindle, an attempt to lay claim to a fortune. Joe Plum's words had held the seeds of reasonable explanation, but even that failed to satisfy. The entire business refused to fit together. There was a wrong to its wrongness, something outside the face of it he couldn't yet pin down.

The soft knock on the door surprised him as it broke into his thoughts and he heard the voice whisper.

"Fargo?" it said through the closed door. "Can I come in? Are you decent?"

He pushed up on one elbow and drew the sheet over his groin. "More or less," he said, and his eyes were on the door as it pushed open. He saw the brown curls first, then Penelope's medium-brown eyes and her quiet face as she came in and pushed the door closed behind her. She wore the dark-blue cotton nightdress, he noted as she halted beside the bed. He watched as her eyes moved across his body, taking in the smooth beauty of his muscled form, before she pulled her gaze to his face.

"You're not very decent."

"As decent as I'm going to get," he answered, and held her in a steady gaze.

"Surprised?" she asked with a trace of coyness.

"Yes," he admitted. "What're you doing here?"

"I decided I wanted to come see you," Penelope said. "There are things I want to talk about."

"I'm listening," he said.

"First, I'm sorry I got so angry earlier," she said.

"You weren't the only one," he said wryly.

She made a face. "Well, they were just putting on an act for you," she said.

"But not you," he said.

"No, not me," she said firmly. "I can see why you might question the letter. You're right, it doesn't really explain everything."

"It doesn't explain anything, honey," he corrected. "Don't try to slide around it."

"All right, maybe it doesn't pin down anything," she admitted. "But even so, I know that letter means just what it says. I know my father wrote it to me," she said.

"How do you know that?" Fargo questioned.

She shrugged, and the medium breasts lifted under the top of the nightgown. "I just do. Something inside," Penelope said.

"Intuition? Sixth sense? Or just wanting to believe it?" he slid at her.

"Call it whatever you like, but I know it. That's why

I want you to help me prove it. Not just for me, but for yourself. I want you to believe in me," Penelope said, her brown eyes very serious. She lowered herself to the edge of the bed, and he smelled the faintly musky scent of her, no powder or perfume, just female, and he felt himself stir under the sheet.

"Please?" she said, and her hand reached to touch his shoulder. "You saved my life. It's important you believe in me," she said. Her eyes moved down across his body again, lingered, almost caressed, paused where the sheet lay across his groin as it moved suddenly. She pulled her gaze back to his face with an effort, and he saw the tiny spots of color touch her cheeks. But her hand stayed on his shoulder.

His smile was wry. "You wanting or bargaining?" he asked.

She thought for a moment. "I'm not sure. Does it matter?" she asked.

"It will to you," Fargo said evenly.

"That'll be my problem, then," she said. Her hands came up, touched the wide straps of the nightdress, and slid them from her shoulders. The garment fell around her waist, and her breasts pushed out at him, curving just enough at the bottoms to give depth, tiny pink nipples in the center of equally pink circles. She rose to her knees at the edge of the bed, and the nightgown fell away entirely, and he took in her nakedness as she stayed on her knees.

One of the medium girls, he had decided when he first saw her, and that didn't change any as she faced him without clothes. But everything was in balance, shoulders, breasts, hips, legs, all of a part, even to the medium-black, modest little triangular nap that covered the tiny pubic mound. There was a quiet, balanced loveliness to her, he realized, an ordered, neat kind of beauty that was terribly attractive in its own way. He sat up and the sheet fell away. He knew he was growing, expanding with desire set loose. Penelope's glance went down to him, and he heard the tiny gasp fall from her lips. Then he was pulling her to him and she felt very small. But her mouth answered his kiss with instant eagerness, opening for him, drawing him in, and her hands slid along the sides of his face. She let her tongue dart forward, and he felt her breasts brush his chest, the tiny tips soft points where they touched his skin.

His fingers curled under one breast, encompassed its modest softness, and he lowered his face to the pink tip, letting his tongue circle the areola with tantalizing slowness.

Penelope sighed. "Ah . . . good, so good."

She lay back, her slender waist arching up as his hand explored the lean flatness of her abdomen, moved down to the curly nap, and pushed slowly through it. Her little cry was instant as he touched the already moistened lips and stroked gently, and he felt her hands dig into his back. She began to move her pelvis, a slow, upward motion, settled back down again, and rose up at once. His hand moved into the dark moistness, and she cried out with delight.

He drew one breast deep into his mouth as he caressed the lubricious lips below, and Penelope's smallish, balanced body half-twisted and rose up in pleasure. "Take me, God, Fargo, take me," she murmured, and he turned and came atop her. His hot, pulsating organ came down across the modest nap, and she cried out again at the touch. She pushed back, lifted, eagerly seeking him. He lowered his hips, came forward, and slid smoothly into her moistened embrace. Penelope screamed, a sharp cry of shuddering pleasure. He was large for her and felt himself rest against the very end of the warm passage as she drew back and thrust forward, crying out in pleasure at each hard thrust. He felt her pressing tight around him as he filled her completely. She pushed up to match his every slow sliding motion.

"God, God, oh, so good, oh, oh," Penelope gasped out, and her words become staccato little bursts of breath at his every sensuous incursion. He felt the sudden tightening around him, the soft walls contracting, even before she began to gasp out.

"Oh, oh, yes, now, now . . . my God," Penelope cried as her tight body stiffened and she slammed her pubic mound hard against him, held there as the climax swept over her. The cry he heard was a small downward arching sound, as filled with dismay as it was with ecstasy. "More, more, oh, damn, more," Penelope said as she gave a last shudder of pleasure and grasped at him, held him tight against her to try to make time hold still.

But the shuddered pleasure slipped into infinity, and Penelope fell back on the bed. She lay still as her arms stayed around his neck. He held inside her until finally he fell away and turned onto his back. She came atop him at once, legs lifting to curl around him, arms across his chest as she held on to him with the tightness of a limpet on a rock. He let his hand move up and down the small of her back and caress the smooth hollow there, then move down to slide across the small, tight rear.

"God, that was good," Penelope whispered against his face. "I wish I could stay."

"Best not," he agreed, and she finally pushed herself to a sitting position, managing to look demure in her naked, balanced loveliness. She reached over and drew the nightdress on, and when she finished, he went to the door with her. She clung to him, her lips finding his mouth again.

"Believe in me, Fargo. Help me. Trust me," she murmured.

"We'll see," he said as he let her go and she slipped into the dark corridor. He closed the door and returned to stretch across the bed, and the smile that touched his lips was wry. The wanting had been real enough, but there was more to it, of course. She'd refused to admit it to him, and perhaps even to herself, but she'd sought to make bed and believing into one and the same for him. Little Penelope had surprised him, though, he admitted, even as he realized that perhaps he shouldn't have been surprised. There was a quiet doggedness about her that was cloaked by the very mediumness of her. She had used words first and then the oldest of methods to make him believe in her. Desperate sincerity or clever calculation? he wondered. But enjoyable, he murmured as he closed his eyes and drew sleep around him, and that alone made it a refreshing change. He turned off thoughts and slept soundly through the remainder of the night.

Morning came in warm with a bright sun, and he allowed himself an extra half-hour of sleep. When he woke, he washed, dressed, and took out time to clean his six-gun before he left the room. The smell of fresh coffee drifted down the corridor, and he found a large enamel coffeepot in the living room along with thick china cups and a tray of sourdough biscuits. The three young women were seated in the room, carefully measured spaces between each. Pepper held a coffeecup in one hand, Penny with an empty cup before her, and Penelope sitting alone and aloof.

" 'Morning," Fargo said, and received only cool silence.

"Did you do your thinking?" Pepper asked sharply.

"Not enough," he said.

"You've seen the letters. I don't know what more there is to think about," Pepper returned, waspishness in her tone.

"There's always more," he said evenly, and saw a flash of smugness touch Penelope's quiet face.

"Are you going to take us to see Judge Stoner?" Penny asked firmly.

"In time," he answered.

"When will that be?" she snapped with disapproval in her face.

"After I think some more," he said.

"It seems you're just dragging your feet." Penny sniffed.

"I'll stop when I'm convinced I'm doing the right thing," Fargo said, and strode to the door. "I'll be back. Meanwhile, I'd stay right here if I were you."

"I'm not going anywhere," Penelope said almost sweetly.

The other two didn't say anything, more out of irritation than any plans to leave, he was certain.

He left the house, saddled the Ovaro, and gave the horse water. He had just finished when Joe Plum appeared on the sturdy-legged pony. Fargo climbed onto the pinto and swung alongside Joe as they headed back toward town.

"Kept thinking about those letters last night. Didn't come up with a damn answer, though," Joe said. "Anybody make a mistake yet?"

Fargo smiled thoughtfully. "Not exactly a mistake," he said. "Just an unexpected move." Joe cast a sidelong glance his way and gave a little snort that said more than words. "I'm still wondering who brought me out here and why. Got any thoughts on that?" Fargo asked.

"Not a damn one," Joe said. "But I keep thinking that if we get one thing answered right, the rest will fall into place."

"Could be," Fargo agreed.

"What've you got in mind for Gordon MacNiff?" Joe asked.

"Put enough fear in him to make him think hard about anything else he might want to do," Fargo said.

"He always has a few of his boys with him," Joe warned.

"They ask for trouble, they'll find it," Fargo growled as the buildings of Otisville came into sight.

"I'd guess MacNiff will be at the general store by now," Joe said, and Fargo put the Ovaro into a canter.

He reached the edge of town and threaded the horse down the main street until he reached the general store and slowed to a halt. A one-horse Owensboro farm wagon with iron hubs was pulled up in front of the loading platform. Fargo saw two men put the last of a row of feedbags into the bed of the wagon. Joe Plum nodded to Fargo, and the Trailsman slid from his horse. He came up behind the two men as they stood beside the wagon and drew the Colt from its holster.

"You boys drop your guns," he said quietly, and both men half-turned, staring at the six-gun trained on them. They hesitated, and Fargo's voice stayed low. "No fool moves. I'm not here for killing. Don't press me," he said. Slowly, the men reached for their guns and tossed them on the ground.

"You must be crazy, mister," one man said, a black kerchief around his neck, heavy black eyebrows over black eyes.

"Maybe. Meanwhile, you two get in that water trough over there," Fargo said.

"What?" The man frowned and started to protest further, but Fargo pulled the hammer back on the Colt.

"Into the trough. Both of you," he ordered, and the two men were wise enough to read the danger in his eyes. Cursing, they moved to the trough, stepped into it, and stood in the almost waist-high water.

"Son of a bitch," the one with the black kerchief swore.

Passing figures began to edge away, and the two men glared at him, but Fargo remained ice-calm. The two men wouldn't be able to make any quick moves from inside the trough, and that's all he wanted. His eyes were on the storefront as the man stepped out, a big man with wide shoulders, clothed in a blue shirt with hide fringes. He bore a large, beaked nose, pale-blue eyes, and a hard mouth that turned down at the corners. He wore an Allen and Wheelock army revolver with a pearl handle, Fargo noted, and he saw Joe Plum nod out of the corner of his eye.

"MacNiff," Fargo called out, and the man turned to

fix him with a commanding stare across the large, beaked nose. "The name's Fargo," the Trailsman said.

Gordon MacNiff reacted instinctively, and his hand yanked at the pistol in its holster. He had it just cleared of the top edge of the holster when Fargo's shot exploded and the Allen and Wheelock flew out of the man's hand.

"Ow, Jesus," said MacNiff as he pulled his stinging hand back.

Fargo fired again, instantly, and this time the shot clipped off the top of Gordon MacNiff's ear. "Jesus Christ," MacNiff screamed as he clapped one hand to the side of his head. Fargo followed with another shot, and this one slammed downward into the side of the man's foot. Gordon MacNiff went down with another shout of pain, rolled, and cursed as Fargo's next two shots followed him, one grazing his ribs, the other drawing a line of blood down the side of his forehead.

Gordon MacNiff came up against the outside wall of the store, his eyes a mixture of fear and surprise as he stared up at the big man who stood over him.

"Any one of those could have killed you, MacNiff," Fargo said. "And maybe they should have. But I'm going to be good to you, though God knows why." He moved a step closer. "The next time you send anybody after me, or any of those gals, you're a dead man, MacNiff. You hear me, mister?" The man stared back, a torrent of emotions rushing through his eyes. "One warning. This is it," Fargo said. "Once more and you're dead. Count on it."

Fargo flicked a glance at the two men in the trough where they stood looking on, and he stepped back to the Ovaro as Gordon MacNiff pushed himself to his feet. Fargo holstered his gun as he swung onto the pinto, nodded to Joe Plum, and turned the horse away from the scene. He had gone perhaps a half-dozen yards when he heard the water splash out of the trough, and he cursed silently. He'd been listening for the sound, knew what it meant, and had hoped not to hear it. But he had, and he whirled in the saddle, the Colt in his hand instantly. The man with the black kerchief was on the ground where he'd landed, one hand scooping up the gun. He turned to fire, but the Colt barked first. The heavy slug slammed into the half-bent figure and the man flew backward and sideways at the same time. He landed half under the trough where the drops of water that dripped from the sides turned red as they fell onto him.

Fargo turned and rode on, not hurrying his pace.

"I'd say you made your point," Joe Plum said.

"For now. MacNiff's not the kind to give up, but he'll draw back a spell, and that's all I want now. Doc Elkins next," Fargo said.

"Straight ahead, small white house near the end of town," Joe said.

Fargo spotted the place after they'd gone on a short while. A light pony rig rested outside the door, and as he drew up, a round-faced man wearing a black frock coat emerged from the house, a black physician's bag in one hand. Gray hair surrounded the round face which showed its age by the tiny little lines around the tired eyes.

"Howdy, Doc," Joe said. "This here is Skye Fargo."

The man nodded. "Heard you've been in town," Doc Elkins said, his tired eyes taking in the big man.

"What can I do for you? I'm on my way to the Landers place."

"Just a question about Clarence Peabody," Fargo said. "You told him he hadn't long to live, and he jumped off that gorge some three months ago."

"That's right," Doc Elkins said.

"Could he have gone on longer?" Fargo asked.

Doc Elkins stared at him with a small frown of thought. "Anything's possible, I wouldn't think much longer, but some men can live with a lot of pain. Some men can do things others can't," the doctor said. "Anything else?"

"Not now," Fargo said. "Much obliged."

Doc Elkins nodded and slowly lifted himself into the pony rig. He drove away, and Fargo slowly headed out of town, Joe Plum riding beside him.

"Tell me more about Clarence Peabody," Fargo said to the old miner. "I want to know about the man himself."

Joe Plum frowned into space as he pulled on memories. "Clarence Peabody kept mostly to himself, never had any real friends. He was a hard man, some said an unprincipled man, and I'd guess they had a point. He made a lot of enemies in his time. When he was younger and Missouri still a territory, he practically ran this part of the country. He was the power and the law then. He did what he wanted, when he wanted to, and how he wanted to. Things changed some when statehood came along, but then Clarence had grown older, too."

"You said it's generally thought he hid away a fortune. Was he a miser? Was he a sour man who hated the world? What kind of man was he?" Fargo asked.

"I wouldn't say he was a sour man. He didn't hate

the world. Contempt, that's a better word. Clarence Peabody had contempt for most people." Joe went on, "He was a real cautious man in business, always covered his own bets. Once he had three freight lines haul ore for him because he refused to depend on any one outfit. It cost him more than if he'd used just one line, but that way none of them could dictate terms to him. He never gave anything away. Clarence Peabody believed that if you wanted anything important, you had to win it, earn it, or fight for it."

"He ever marry?"

"Never. Had any woman he wanted, but he never married," Joe said, and cast a sidelong glance at the big man. "What are all these questions and that one you tossed at Doc Elkins? What is it you're thinking?" he asked.

"I've been wondering if Clarence Peabody set this all up to have the last laugh. What if he never jumped off that ledge?" Fargo offered.

"Try again. Clarence jumped. They found his body at the bottom of the gorge, downstream a few miles," Joe said.

Fargo swore softly. "Damn. That blows that idea away," he bit out.

"Figure out the girls first. One answer could lead to another," Joe said, and Fargo nodded agreement.

"What do you know about Judge Stoner?" he asked.

"He used to be a small-time town judge. When statehood came, he got lucky and was made a county judge. He's not much, but he's the only judge in the county," Joe said.

"Was he a friend of Clarence Peabody?" Fargo queried.

"No more than most folks," Joe said as Fargo turned the Ovaro up into the hills. He led the way high up along the back line of the hills to finally emerge high on a crag that overlooked the mine below. "You going to tell the girls they all have the same letter?" Joe asked.

"Not for now. I want more time. Maybe one of them will slip up, drop her guard, make a mistake. Maybe more than one will," Fargo said.

"They'll be wanting you to take them to see Judge Stoner," Joe said.

"I'll try to hold that off some," Fargo said, and began to move slowly down the hillside. As they reached halfway down the side of the hills, they began to pass the boarded-up mine-shaft entrances.

"Some folks have always thought Clarence stowed his fortune away in one of his mine shafts," Joe said.

"Never, not that man you've described to me. There'd have been too much of a chance for someone to come onto it or see him doing it. He wouldn't have hidden it anywhere near here," Fargo said.

"You're probably right," Joe agreed. "Maybe where nobody's ever going to find it."

Fargo allowed a grim snort. "All this sweating over a prize that may never be found," he said. The irony of it had a bitter edge as he thought of a thousand-dollar promise that might never be kept. As he rode down into the flatland below, the three figures took shape outside the house. Penny sat on a wood chair, her head tilted back as she dried her jet-black hair. Pepper and Penelope took turns at a big, round wash pail with their wash. Penelope busily shook water from a black skirt she then carefully folded over a piece of planking that lay in the sun.

Fargo watched Joe Plum stare at the three young women with a narrowed glance. "Talk to me, Joe," he said.

"I keep thinking they've all got to be faking it," Joe said. "No other way to explain their all having the same letter. Just a slip-up someplace."

"You could be right," Fargo admitted, and knew that though he had no better explanation, something inside him still hung back, refused acceptance with its own, hidden reasons. "Scout around some more, Joe," he said. "Keep an eye on MacNiff's place if you can. I expect he'll lay low for a spell, but I'd like to be sure."

"I'll look in on him," Joe said. "Stop by in the morning."

"Good enough," Fargo said, and Joe rode away with a wave of his hand. Fargo rode on to the house, dismounted, and stabled the Ovaro in the nearby barn. When he returned, Pepper and Penelope had gone into the house, but Penny still sat outside and began to brush the thick, luxurious jet locks.

Fargo watched her and enjoyed the way her white, cotton blouse pulled tight as the deep, round breasts rose and fell with each brushing movement of her arm.

He took his eyes from her and spied the outdoor bucket shower that sat at the corner of the house. He walked to it, saw the overhead bucket was filled, and stepped behind the small, square of wood that served as a makeshift stall. He undressed quickly, put his clothes outside on the ground, and when he straightened, the piece of wood hardly rose to his hips. He turned the spigot on at the bottom of the bucket and reveled in the cool, clean water that cascaded over him. When he finished, he reached down, wrapped his shirt around his hips, and stepped from the shower. His body glistened with droplets of water, and the beauty and power of his figure was heightened by the wetness under the sun. He found a patch of grass and lay down, but not before he saw Penny watching him, her eyes moving up and down his body. She had all but stopped brushing her hair. He smiled inwardly as he felt her eyes stay on him while he relaxed in the sun.

He heard her stir finally, looked aside, and saw her get up. She threw a last glance back at him as she walked to the house, and he stayed under the sun until his skin dried. He rose, put on clothes and gun belt as the sun dropped behind the mountain crags to signal the close of the day. He walked into the house and saw Asa Toomey in the entranceway, her face stiff as the broom handle she held in her hand.

"Stew's on for the taking," she said, paused, and shot a narrowed glance at him. "How long you going to go on with this damnfool business?" the woman asked.

"Meaning what?" He frowned.

"Three Penelope Julia Peabodys." She sniffed derisively. "When there's not even one."

"You know that for sure?" Fargo asked quickly.

"Never heard of one. Never saw one," the woman grunted.

"Doesn't mean there isn't one. Clarence Peabody was a rich man. You can buy a lot with money, people, silence—almost anything," Fargo said.

"Pick any one of them," Asa Toomey said. "It's time to get this over with."

"Why? Does time make any difference to you?" Fargo asked sharply.

The woman shrugged. "Only that I'm not staying on much longer. My time's up soon. I won't be around cookin' and cleanin'," she said.

"This'll be over long before then," Fargo said, and the woman walked away with another shrug.

He watched her go, and her words turned again in his mind. Asa Toomey seemed a shade too interested, her practical answer notwithstanding. He wondered again whether her commitment to Clarence Peabody's in-advance wages was the only reason she had stayed. Perhaps Asa Toomey had thoughts of something more. Maybe she'd spent every day trying to find Clarence Peabody's fortune. Maybe she still wanted to be on hand if it were found.

He put away idle thoughts and strolled into the kitchen, sat down with a plate and some stew, and ate hungrily. He had just finished when Pepper came in. "I'd have waited if I'd known you were coming," Fargo said.

She tossed him a cold stare as she took a plate of the stew. "I don't eat with people who refuse to believe the truth when they see it," she said loftily, and strode from the room. He watched her slender figure, tight rear, narrow waist that emphasized the slight sway of her lean hips.

He stayed in the kitchen for a while, but no one else appeared, and he finally put away his plate and left. The night stayed warm and he kept the lamp out in his room as he undressed and lay down. Once more, thoughts quickly slid through his mind, all the unexplainable factors that didn't make sense even from the viewpoint of a swindle. Asa Toomey said there'd never been a real Penelope Julia Peabody, and Joe Plum saw all three girls as fakes, part of a scheme that had somehow gone awry. Maybe they were right, Fargo pondered and felt annoyed at himself for the undefined feeling inside himself that continued to hold back.

He was pushing thoughts aside almost angrily when he heard the faint knock at the door. "May I come in?" the voice whispered through the door. Fargo held still a moment before answering. His hand drew the sheet up, then hesitated. There was no need if it were Penelope again. But she'd made her pitch. There was no reason for her to return, except desire. He drew the sheet over himself, suddenly uncertain.

"It's open," he said, and the door pushed in.

The figure entered, a floor-length white nightgown with a deep-cut neckline, cut full yet unable to hide the round curves of the body inside it. Its whiteness contrasted against the jet-black thick hair that hung down to her shoulders. Penny closed the door behind her and stepped toward him, her eyes quickly sweeping his near-naked body. He watched her with a half-smile as she halted beside him, black-brown eyes returning slowly to his face.

"I came because I want to talk to you alone," she said, her voice soft, low, almost purring.

"Thought you were disappointed in me," Fargo remarked.

Her full red lips tightened for an instant. "I *was* disappointed in you," she admitted. "And that made me angry."

"I haven't changed my mind any," Fargo said.

"Maybe I can help you see things differently," Penny said, and took a step closer to where he lay on the bed. He'd been honest with Penelope. He'd be no less now.

"You can try. You can't buy," he said.

The black-brown eyes held his gaze. "I know that," she said firmly.

He smiled inwardly. She did know that, he was certain, and it wouldn't make a damn bit of difference. Another part of her had to try, the part that refused to admit her special female powers wouldn't work. He tossed a half-shrug at her.

"So long as you know," he said, and Penny lowered herself on the edge of the bed and he watched the deep, very round breasts sway under the neckline of the nightgown.

"My letter isn't a fake. It wasn't written as part of some swindle," she said.

"It sure doesn't prove anything," Fargo said.

"That's exactly it. A fake letter would be full of the kind of details you'd call proof," Penny said. "A fake letter would be certain to offer up some kind of proof."

Fargo felt himself frowning. She was making a kind of reverse sense. "Maybe," he admitted. "Or maybe no proof is better than phony proof.

"There's more," Penny said. "Ma once mentioned my father to me, long ago. She said he was a rich man, but that'd never do me any good."

"Anything else?" Fargo queried.

"She told me he was a man who said he'd always live his life his way," Penny answered. "Don't you see? That's what he said in his letter, the very exact words. That has to mean something."

Fargo let his lips purse. "Maybe," he allowed.

"But not enough to make you believe in me," Penny said.

"I'll think more on it," he allowed.

"Is that all?" She frowned.

"That's all," he said. "I guess that means you can go now."

Her black-brown eyes stayed on him, and she didn't move. "What if I don't want to go?" she asked.

"I'm not figuring to talk more," Fargo said.

"I'm not either," Penny said, and leaned forward. She bent down and stopped when the deep breasts all but spilled from the neckline of her nightgown. She stayed motionless. It was pure teasing, he knew, and he brushed inside the jet locks to close his hand around the back of her neck. He pulled her to him roughly, and Penny's full red lips parted at once, her kiss warm and wet and full of throbbing desire. His hand came up to push against one very deep breast and felt its softness flow around his fingers. She pulled back, crossed her arms, and lifted the nightgown from her as she rested on her knees beside him. The very round, deep breasts gushed forward, flat, very light-pink tips that seemed even flatter and smaller on the heavy mounds. Small, equally light-pink circles surrounded each and, despite their size, gave her breasts a pastel quality. Her waist, a little thick, flowed into wide hips and a very dark, tangly triangle. Full-fleshed thighs seemed to vibrate with their own energy.

Penny came to him, almost threw herself atop him. He fell back and let the full breasts press against him, their softness pillowlike. He pushed his face into the deep cleft between them. Penny gave a half-sigh, moved and pushed one breast over his face, pressed the almost flat tip against his lips. He drew on it, caressed with his tongue, and she sighed again as the tiny tip remained almost flat.

His hands ran down Penny's back, across the layer of extra flesh she wore with the ease of youth, down to her ample rear, and squeezed. Penny grunted and slid half off him. He turned, found the other deep breast with his hand, and cupped its fullness as he ran his thumb across the light-pink tip. Penny's hips moved, half-twisted, and Fargo let his hand slide down across the convex curve of her belly, push into the tangled triangle.

Penny gasped with anticipation as he slid his hand down farther, pressed it into the fullness of her thighs, fleshed out fully yet without any flab. She kept her thighs together and surprised him, and he pressed deeper, neared the tip of the tangled triangle as he brought his hand upward. "Oh," she breathed as her legs suddenly relaxed, fell open, and came together again around his hand in a fleshy vise. She held him there for a long moment until he pressed again, and he felt her thighs relax, fall open, and his hand came up against the warm, moist darkness.

Penny's cry was sudden, eagerness again in the sound, and her arm came around his neck, pushed his face hard into one pillowy breast. He opened his lips, nibbled on the deep mound as he let his fingers move slowly, touch, pause, touch again. "Ah, yes, ah, ah," Penny moaned, the sound a guttural one from the back of her throat. He moved suddenly, swiftly, almost harshly, into the warm funnel as he caressed the very full lips.

"Oh, my God, oh," Penny cried out, and he felt her hips lift, slowly twist, fall back again.

Her hand reached for him, slid down his leg, and came to the throbbing warmth of him. She cried out in delight as she found him, then half-turned toward him, her body seeking, the portal welcoming. He rose onto his knees, turned, brought himself down atop the tangled triangle.

Penny cried out again and lifted, her ample hips rising high as she sought him. He drew back and came forward, a sliding thrust that slipped smoothly into the warm glove. Penny's cry was a groaning, moaning sound that came from somewhere deep inside her belly, rose in power and intensity as he slid forward and back again and forward once more.

He let his rhythm develop, and Penny's little belly jiggled against him as she lifted with his slow, smooth plunging, each a tiny bit faster. "Ah, yes, ah, ah, my God, ah," Penny gasped, and her head began to turn from side to side, the ink-jet locks flailing against the bedsheet with glistening blackness.

Suddenly, as though an explosion of energy had swept through her, her thighs began to fall away and come together against him, pressing, striking into his hips as her slightly chunky torso lifted, rose higher, thrust upward, and fell back only to almost leap upward again. She began to cry out, deep groaning gasps with her every motion. The round creamy pillows bounced in rhythm. Her arms pulled against his shoulders, and suddenly she was all gasped groans and fervent, shaking flesh, a torrid little volcano of desire.

"Go on, go on, more, oh, God, more," Penny groaned and cried out and half-moaned as she tossed the halo of jet locks back and forth. She pulled his face down to the bouncing, swaying pillowed mounds even as she pushed her chunky pelvis hard against him, matching his thrusting with her own almost frantic motions.

"Fargo," he heard her cry out suddenly, a sharp abruptness in her voice, almost a fear. *"Fargo!"* she screamed again, her voice rising a half-octave. Her shaking body rose, seemed to freeze itself in midair, and the groaning sound came from her in a coarse spiral. Her thighs were tight around him, pressing hard into his waist as her climax seized her in its overwhelming totality.

"Ah, God," Penny breathed at the end of her orgasm, the words coming at the edge of a long, breathy sigh that held both fulfillment and dismay. She sank down onto the bed with her legs still around him until slowly they fell away, and he rolled to his side next to her.

She lay, breathing heavily, the deep breasts falling to one side as she half-turned to face him. He took in her body, saw the tiny pale-pink tips remained almost flat on the round breasts. But though she lay satiated and still, her firm, rounded body still exuded a dormant energy. She stretched, laid her breasts across his chest.

"I'd like to stay," Penny said.

"Fine with me," Fargo said.

"No, they wouldn't understand. They'd think the wrong thing right away," she said, and pulled herself up.

"Guess so," Fargo said blandly.

Penny swung from the bed and drew the white nightgown on. She clung to him a moment longer as he stood up beside her. "Thanks for listening," she said with a gratefulness that seemed completely honest, and her kiss was as soft and tender as it was quick.

She hurried from the room and he was alone. He stretched across the bed again and the word fell softly from his lips. "Damn," he murmured. He had felt the same sincerity in Penny as he had in Penelope the night before. Behind trying their female weapons they seemed to believe in the words. Or were they both that good actresses? He grimaced at the thought, unwilling to accept it, unable to reject what he had felt about both. They just refused to fit the picture of clever little swindlers or gullible pawns. Pepper came into his thoughts and he smiled as he wondered if she'd come visiting next. The thought was shattered by the explosion of angry shouts from the living room.

"Whore, that's what you are. Nothing but a whore," he heard the voice and recognized Pepper's icy tones.

"Don't you call me names," he heard Penny fire back. "You were just on your way to peddle your little ass."

"I was not. You just have a dirty mind," Pepper said with icy disdain.

Fargo swung from the bed, pulled on trousers, and hurried from the room. He moved down the corridor on silent steps to see the two young woman facing each other in the living room. A lamp was turned up, and he saw Penny in the loose white nightgown and Pepper with a brown cotton robe wrapped around her slender figure. He halted in the shadows of the corridor as Penelope appeared and stepped into the room.

"What's all the shouting?" she asked, rubbed sleep from her eyes.

"This whore was in with Fargo, peddling her favors for his," Pepper said with an accusing stare at Penny. "I just caught her coming away from his room."

"Where you were heading?" Penny snapped.

"I was going to the kitchen for some water," Pepper shouted, and turned to Penelope. Fargo saw the frown flood her face as she stared at Penelope. "You don't seem very bothered," she said.

"Oh, sure, I'm bothered," Penelope said, but her recovery wasn't quick enough.

"No, you were only a little surprised. You went to him already, didn't you?" Pepper said.

"I went to talk to him," Penelope said.

"That's all I did," Penny put in.

"Liar," Penelope shot back at her.

"Same to you," Penny snapped.

"You're two of a kind." Pepper frowned. "Whores, both of you."

"Don't play Miss High and Mighty with us," Penny returned.

"I'm going to see about this," Pepper snapped as she whirled to stalk from the room.

Fargo stepped out of the shadows, and she halted, her light-blue eyes filled with turmoil and fury.

"Looking for me?" Fargo said.

Pepper's eyes took in the naked power of his chest, and her eyes darkened. "Bastard," she hissed. "Which one of these whores did you sell out to? Or did you promise them both you'd help them?"

"Didn't promise anybody anything," Fargo said calmly.

"You just slept with them," Pepper flung at him.

"They knew the rules." He shrugged.

"*Hah!*" she snorted. "I'll bet. And I thought you had some principles. You're no better than they are," Pepper shouted, and he saw her eyes fill with tears as she turned and ran from the room. He heard the front door pull open as she ran from the house.

"You two stay here," he ordered with a hard glance at Penny and Penelope, hurried down the hall and set out into the night. He heard her half-running up the slope at the back of the house and he followed, caught sight of her where she halted beside one of the ore carts. He heard her sobs when he reached her.

"Leave me alone," she said, turned her back to him as he approached.

He circled around to face her. The tears on her cheeks were real, he saw, but he decided to press harder. "You pained or provoked?" he asked.

"What's that mean?" She sniffled.

"You all upset with me or just mad because you didn't get to me first?" Fargo clarified.

Her arm came up in a wild swing, and he pulled his head back easily. "Damn you," she hissed.

"Easy, honey," Fargo said. "Now try answering the question."

"I wouldn't want to get to you that way, first or last," Pepper said. "I just thought you were different. When you saved my life in that mine shaft, I thought maybe you were honest about wanting to get at the truth."

"I am," Fargo said.

"By sleeping with those two?" Pepper flung back. "By letting a pair of eager legs buy you?"

"Nobody's bought me," Fargo said.

114

Her eyes glared at him. "I can't believe that. I can't believe anything anymore," she said.

"That makes two of us," Fargo said with sudden harshness. "Now, you've done enough fussin' for one night. Get back to the house."

"Is that all you have to say?"

"For now," he answered, and turned away from her. He paused, waited, and she walked down the slope beside him. The brown robe moved as she walked, and he glimpsed the side of one longish breast. He frowned as he walked. She had wrapped herself in anger and something more. The kind of bitterness he felt from her was not something that could be feigned. She had only added to what he felt about the other two. A strange, deep streak of sincerity held each of them. Or they were a trio of the best damn actresses he'd ever met.

Penelope and Penny were sitting almost at opposite ends of the living room when he returned with Pepper.

"Back so soon?" Penny slid out waspishly.

"Jealous or curious?" Pepper threw back.

"I've a few things about being honest to say to you, Fargo," Penny put in.

"After me," Penelope said.

Fargo swept the three young women with a cold glance. "You can all have your say, come morning," he said, spun on his heel, and strode from the room. He shut the door loudly, shed trousers, and lay down on the bed. Pepper's outburst had only reinforced the feelings he couldn't shake. Her very real bitterness and tears didn't fit the picture of a clever little swindler any more than Penny and Penelope fit the picture. He closed his eyes and drew a deep breath.

It was time to let the mind float of itself in sleep. He would draw in every detail he knew, everything that had happened, everything Joe Plum had told him, every opinion anyone had voiced, including himself. Thoughts would swim through his head while he slept, sort themselves out in their own mysterious ways. They would find their own places, come together in their own ways, and maybe he'd find an answer. It had happened before for him, the mind set free to do its own seeking, unrestrained by conscious logic or imposed reasoning. He lay very still and let sleep sweep over him to shut out the world.

The night stayed warm and still, and he slept soundly in the silent dark. The hours rolled on slowly and were edging the dawn when he suddenly woke and sat bolt upright in bed. His eyes snapped open as he stared into the darkness.

"That's it," he said out loud. "Goddamn, that has to be it."

He sat upright for a moment longer, his head pounding, and then fell back onto the bed, his eyes closed at once. The mind had drawn all the random things together as he slept, sleep offered explanations and answers that had eluded the conscious mind. He'd not probe now, not pick and question. He'd wait for morning to add one more confirmation to the answer that had spiraled into place as he slept. He turned on his side, drew sleep around him again, and for the first time since he'd arrived, he slept with answers inside himself instead of only questions.

116

# 5

He was dressed and waiting in the living room with a mug of coffee when they came in one by one. Pepper was first, in a cool, light-green blouse and black skirt. Penny was next, in riding britches and a white cotton blouse, her flat cheekbones drawn tight. Penelope was last and looked quietly contained, but he caught anxiety in her brown eyes. She edged herself onto a chair, her eyes on him.

"Go on, tell us," she said. "What have you decided?"

"First take out your letters," Fargo said. "Show them to each other."

"I will not." Pepper frowned. "That's private, just for me."

"I'm not showing my letter to them," Penelope said.

He speared Penelope with a hard stare. "Give me the damn letter," he said, and she drew it from the pocket of her skirt and handed it to him. His eyes moved over the three girls again as he held Penelope's letter in front of him. "They're all the same, every

117

damn one of them," he said. "Look at your own while I read." He waited, watched Penny and Pepper frown as they drew their letters out. He began to read Penelope's letter aloud, slowly and distinctly, and watched their frowns turn from surprise to shocked disbelief when he finished.

Penny was first to find her voice. "I—I don't understand," she murmured, words hardly more than a coarse whisper.

"It—it can't be," Pepper said as she stared down at her letter.

"Only it is," Fargo said, and handed the letter back to Penelope. She stared at him with incomprehension as she took the little square of note paper. "The same, all three of them, identical," he said again.

"Is this some kind of sick joke?" Pepper asked. "What does it mean?"

Fargo held back words. He had confirmed only one part of it. They had been as surprised and nonplussed by the revelation as he'd expected. But he had to be sure of the rest before he said anything more to them.

"It means I might have the truth soon," he said. He peered through the window at the sound of a horse approaching and saw Joe Plum ride up. "I'll be back soon as I can. Meanwhile keep your letters to yourselves, just as you've been doing," he said, and started from the room.

Asa Toomey appeared in the hallway with a big pot of coffee.

"They'll be needing that inside," Fargo directed.

Asa Toomey regarded him with narrowed eyes. "You pick out the real one?" she asked.

"Soon," he said as he hurried from the house. Joe Plum had dismounted and walked toward him.

"Come into the barn with me while I saddle up," Fargo said. "Got something for you."

"I'm listening," Joe said.

"We've been looking at this all wrong," Fargo said as he began to saddle the pinto.

"How's that?" Joe asked.

"Wondering if they're all fake or which is the real one," Fargo said. "They're all for real."

"*What?*" Joe Plum frowned in astonishment.

"That's right. It came to me in the night, and strangely, it's the only thing that makes sense out of it," Fargo said as he tightened the cinch.

"You telling me they're all Clarence Peabody's daughters?" Joe Plum frowned.

"That's what I'm saying," Fargo answered. "And he wrote the same letter to each of them."

"Why?" Joe pressed.

"I don't know that yet, but I'm pretty damn sure I'm right. It fits the man, everything you told me about him: his caution, his way of doing things, his past. Those three girls believe in the letters they got. They're not acting out a part, being clever little swindlers, and that fits, too. Of course, that still leaves a lot of questions unanswered."

"Such as who sent for you and why," Joe offered.

"Exactly, but first things first. You said Doc Elkins has been the only doc around these parts for forty years. He ought to be able to pin down the first part about the girls," Fargo said, swung long legs up into the saddle, and rode from the barn. "You stay here with them, keep an eye on things till I get back," he said, and Joe nodded.

Fargo sent the horse across the hollow of land at a fast canter and headed toward Otisville. He lined up questions in his mind as he rode, and the sun had started to dip into the afternoon when he reined up in front of the small white house.

Doc Elkins answered the door, a flicker of surprise in his tired eyes as he saw the big man. "Fargo," he grunted. "More questions about Clarence?"

"More or less," Fargo said.

"Come in," Doc Elkins said, and Fargo followed the man into a waiting room, glimpsed a portly woman seated in an inner office. "Mrs. Dooley will be leaving in a few minutes," the doctor said, and disappeared into the inside office.

Fargo surveyed the waiting room, paused to examine an old stethoscope hung on the wall. A fifty-cent piece in a frame hung nearby. He halted at three crumbling, yellow volumes on a small desk, held together with a thin red ribbon, and saw they were medical texts. A diploma occupied the center of another wall of the waiting room, a room where everything was in place: ashtray, water pitcher, a small note pad with pencil on the desk, everything neat and ordered. Even the feather duster had its own cradle in the corner of the room.

He turned as he heard the door open, and the woman swept through the waiting room and left as Doc Elkins came toward him with a slow smile. "Sorry you had to wait," the man said.

"No bother. Enjoyed looking around your waiting room," Fargo said.

Doc Elkins' smile widened, and he paused before the old stethoscope. "My very first one," he said. "And this fifty-cent piece was my first fee."

"The books?" Fargo inquired.

"The ones I used to go through medical school.

They're a part of me," Doc Elkins said. "Now, what can I do for you, Fargo?"

"I want to know about Clarence Peabody's three daughters," Fargo said.

The man's eyes widened as he stared back. "What are you talking about?" he said.

"Clarence fathered three daughters," Fargo said. "By three different women. Twenty to twenty-five years ago."

The doctor's stare held. "I can't recall Clarence calling on me for anything like that," he said.

"Maybe he didn't. Maybe the three women called you. But three women gave birth to daughters. They had to give the father's name," Fargo said.

"Yes, that's necessary on a birth certificate," the doctor agreed.

"You don't remember?" Fargo questioned.

"No, twenty-five years ago is a long time," Doc Elkins said.

"Your records ought to prove it. One girl was born in 1835, one in '37, and one in '39," Fargo said.

Doc Elkins drew a long breath and allowed a reluctant shrug to lift his shoulders. "I'm sorry. I don't have any records, certainly none going that far back," he said.

"No records?" Fargo frowned in surprise.

"I'm afraid not. I rarely keep any today. I always felt patients were more important than records, and I don't have time for both," Doc Elkins said. "When a woman gives birth, I fill out a proper birth certificate and give it to her. That's all that's required." The doctor stepped toward the door as Fargo's glance swept the room again. "Sorry I can't help you," Doc Elkins said. "Guess you'll have to decide on the right young woman on your own."

"Looks that way," Fargo said. "Thanks for your time." He walked from the house and swung onto the Ovaro outside as the doctor slowly closed the door.

Fargo rode out of town and guided the horse into a thick cluster of white oak, a frown on his brow as he swung from the saddle. The man had lied, Fargo muttered inwardly, and he sat back against a tree trunk. Why? he wondered. But the answer to that would have to wait, he realized. Other things took priority. He wanted a look at the good doctor's files. There would be records, he was certain, and he stretched out under the oaks and let the rest of the day slowly move into dusk.

When night began to roll over the land, he rose, took the horse, and returned to town. He found an empty storage shed that let him see the neat white house with the pony rig outside. He waited patiently as the night deepened, and he straightened in the saddle as the door opened and Doc Elkins came out, his black bag in one hand. The man climbed into the pony rig and drove away.

Fargo stayed in place until the rig disappeared into the darkness at the end of town. He moved forward then, led the Ovaro around to the far side of the house, and dismounted. He tried a window, found it locked, and went on to another that lifted at his touch. He swung his long legs over the windowsill to find himself in the doctor's inner office. Groping carefully, he found a lamp and turned it on low.

He scanned the room, focused on the wooden cabinet against one wall. He opened the top drawer and grunted in satisfaction at the drawer of five-by-five cards, filed in double rows. Each section of cards was indexed by a year marker in proper fashion. He rifled through to 1835 first and began to scan the cards that followed. He read only those with a woman's name at the top and halted when he spotted the name "Rose" on a card. He lifted the card out and read the careful, neat handwriting.

Dalton, Rose
Delivered of baby girl, June 19, 1835
Name: Penelope Julia Peabody
Father: Clarence Peabody

His eyes narrowed in thought, Fargo put the card on the desk and moved on to the section of cards filed under 1837. He rifled through them until he found the one he sought and pulled it from the file as he scanned it:

Montez, Maria
Delivered of baby girl, April 12, 1837
Name: Penelope Julia Peabody
Father: Clarence Peabody

He put the card down on top of the other one on the desk and returned to the file cabinet. The last one proved the most difficult. He hadn't asked Pepper about her mother, and he went through the cards carefully, reading each that bore a woman's name on it. He was almost at the end of the section when he came to the card he searched for. He pulled it out of the file as he read the few lines on it.

Brenner, Martha
Delivered of baby girl, December 20, 1839
Name: Penelope Julia Peabody
Father: Clarence Peabody

Fargo put the third card with the other two, closed the cabinet, and turned the lamp off. With the cards in the pocket of his jacket, he made his way from the room and pulled the window down when he left. He led the Ovaro along the back of the house and cut into the woods as he stayed clear of the road. He pressed the cards in his pocket in satisfaction. He had been right about the letters and the three young women. But it was all still surrounded by strange and unanswered questions, and now there was a new one added. Why had the good doctor lied about not keeping records? Fargo set the question aside until he made another visit to the man and hurried the Ovaro through the night.

Lights were still on when he reached the big house, Joe Plum's pony still at the hitching post outside. Fargo put the Ovaro into the barn and went into the house. Joe sat in the living room with the three women. His wrinkled face held quizzical curiosity while the girls' mirrored uncertainty and apprehension. Fargo's eyes circled the three of them. "You'd best start being nice to each other, seeing as you're all sisters," he remarked, and watched their mouths drop open almost as one. "Half-sisters, to be correct about it," he added.

He took the file cards from his pocket, handed them to Penny, and waited and watched as she passed them to the others. He cast a glance at Joe Plum.

"Still mighty strange," the little man said. "Still leaves a damn lot of things to fit in."

"It surely does," Fargo said, and told him how Doc Elkins had claimed he kept no records. "Know any reasons why he'd do that?" Fargo asked.

Joe shook his head slowly, almost sadly. "Not a

124

damn one," he murmured. "You'll face him with it, won't you?"

"In time. First, we pay Judge Stoner a visit tomorrow," he said, returned his eyes to the three girls.

"I still don't understand it," Penelope said, her quiet face even more composed than usual. "Why did he send for all three of us? Why write the very same letter to each of us?"

"Don't know that yet," Fargo said. "But he did, and that makes all three of you heir to whatever fortune there is. You'll split it three ways."

"That's fine with me," Pepper said. "If it's a lot, there'll be plenty for each of us. If it's not much, it'll still be more than we have now."

"I'll second that," Penny said.

Penelope stared at the card in her hand for a moment. "Why did he name us all the same?" She frowned.

Joe Plum's voice cut in. "That fits old Clarence," he said. "When he liked a name, he kept using it. He had four horses over the years that he named Blaze. It's the kind of thing that would appeal to his strange sense of humor, too."

"I expect more answers will be popping up. We go to see Judge Stoner first thing in the morning," Fargo said. "Get yourselves some sleep now."

Penelope nodded, turned to Pepper, and paused awkwardly for a moment. Then she stepped toward her, and Pepper's long, lean figure responded to the embrace. They turned to Penny and included her as they started to move to the corridor.

"They'll be needing each other for support," Joe murmured. "It's a whole new world for them." He turned to the door. "I'll bed down outside."

"Plenty of room in here," Fargo said.

"Never could get used to sleeping indoors on a warm night. See you, come morning," the old miner said, and hurried outside.

Fargo went to his room, undressed, and lay across the bed. His own question still remained unanswered. Who had sent for him and why? Maybe Judge Stoner would resolve that, he reflected, and drew sleep around himself. Clarence Peabody had leapt into a gorge to his death, but he seemed more alive than dead.

Fargo slept soundly till morning came, then he rose, washed, and dressed. He met Asa Toomey in the living room as she set down a tray of coffee mugs and the big enamel pot. The woman's cold, expressionless face gazed at him, and her thin line of a mouth hardly moved as she spoke.

"Heard those three chattering in the bathroom this morning," she said. "That true what they're saying? They're all Clarence Peabody's daughters?"

"It is," Fargo said. "Got the proof of it."

"The old bastard," Asa Toomey said as she turned away and walked from the room. She disappeared into the hallway just as Pepper entered, her long, slender figure clothed in a pale-green dress that heightened the auburn in her hair. She shimmered with loveliness as she hurried to him, and her lips were on his before he had a chance to react, a quick, warm touch that ended all too quickly.

"For not writing us off," she said.

"You a delegation of one?" he asked.

"No, that was my idea," she said.

"You're on the right track." He grinned.

Penny and Penelope entered, took coffee, and

waited for him as he finished the hot brew in the mug he held.

"Anything we should say to the judge?" Penelope asked.

"Just show him your letters. I'll show him the doc's records," Fargo said. "Get your horses. I'll meet you outside."

They nodded and left together. Fargo walked outside, scanned the area, and spotted Joe Plum off to one side as he shook out his blanket. He strode to the old miner, who waved at him.

" 'Mornin," Joe said.

"I'm on my way to see Judge Stoner with the girls. Can you follow along and wait outside his office?" Fargo asked. "I may want you to bring the girls back here."

"Sure thing. Soon as I get myself together," Joe said.

"See you there," Fargo said, and strode to the barn. He saddled up quickly, and the three girls were on their mounts and waiting as he rode from the barn. "Let's make time," he said.

He set a pace just fast enough for them to stay within sight of him as he headed toward town, and he slowed only when he reached the edge of town. The pony rig was outside Doc Elkins' office as he rode by, and in the center of town he drew to a halt as he saw the sheriff.

"Where do I find Judge Stoner?" he asked mildly, and saw the curiosity in the man's eyes as he glanced at the three young women.

"Across the street, town courthouse," the sheriff said. "You decide which of these three is for real?"

"They all are," Fargo said. "And they're claiming

Clarence Peabody's estate. You can tell MacNiff that it's over. He's a loser.

Fargo spurred the pinto across the street to where the courthouse sign was almost invisible against a weathered door front, and dismounted. Pepper was first to follow him inside, where a small man in a black frock coat and stiff collar glanced up from a desk. Little blue eyes looked out of a tight, pinched face.

"Judge Stoner?" Fargo asked.

"Yes?" the judge said, and swept the three young women with a sharp-eyed glance.

"Give the judge those letters," Fargo said, and Penny handed hers up first, Pepper and Penelope adding theirs quickly. Fargo waited in silence as the judge read the letters and his frown deepened. When he finished, Fargo gave him the three birth records. The judge's frown grew deeper, and he finally lifted his gaze to the three young woman.

"Are you saying you're all Clarence Peabody's daughters? And you're all named Penelope Julia Peabody?" he asked.

"They're not saying it," Fargo cut in. "The proof is in front of you, cut and dried."

"Never heard of anything like this," Judge Stoner muttered.

"Me neither, but it's still true," Fargo said.

The judge stared at the letters and the birth records again. "Yes, it seems to be," he murmured.

"Why does the letter tell us to come to you?" Penelope asked.

"Your father left a letter in my care for Penelope Julia Peabody if she came to claim it," the judge said.

"I guess there's nothing for me to do but give it to the three of you."

He rose and went to a safe in a corner of the room, took a moment to open it, and returned with a white envelope.

Pepper reached her hand out and he gave it to her. "Thank you," she said, unable to keep a hint of triumph out of her voice.

"I'll have to keep these letters and record cards for my files," the judge said. "After all, this is most unusual."

Fargo watched Pepper exchange glances with Penny and Penelope.

"That's fine with us," she said, and Fargo followed the three young women as they all but ran out of the office.

Outside, he saw Joe Plum just riding up and waved him over as Pepper tore the envelope open with Penny and Penelope looking over her shoulder. Her smooth brow wrinkled as she stared down at the piece of paper and finally lifted her eyes to Fargo.

"I don't understand it," she said. "It doesn't mean anything to me." She pushed the piece of paper at him as Joe Plum came up to look at it with him. Fargo read the only two names written on the sheet aloud.

"Arrow Mountain. Kawaharu," he said.

"Arrow Mountain's in Kansas Territory. Right smack in the middle of Pawnee country," Joe Plum explained.

"And *kawaharu* is the Pawnee word for the sacred, the presence of the great spirit in the world," Fargo said.

"Damn," Joe Plum spit out. "Hot damn." He uttered a wry laugh. "It fits. Damn if it doesn't."

"Fit's what?" Penelope questioned.

"Fits your pa. Fits Clarence Peabody right down to the bone," Joe said.

"Which means what to us?" Pepper frowned.

"Trouble, that's what it means for you. Trouble," the old miner said. He turned his eyes to Fargo. "Remember I told you that Clarence believed that if you wanted anything important, you had to win it, earn it, or fight for it?" he said.

"Yes, I remember," Fargo said as another piece of the puzzle fell into place. "That's where he hid his fortune, somewhere on Arrow Mountain in the middle of Pawnee country."

"That has to be it," Joe agreed. "It's there someplace for you, a gift you'll have to earn or fight for."

"How could we ever find it, much less get it?" Pepper asked.

"You couldn't. That's why I'm here," Fargo put in.

"But he didn't send for you, and neither did we," Penny said.

"Somebody did," Fargo said.

"Somebody who figured you were the only one with a chance to find the fortune, and he wanted you on hand," Joe added.

Fargo felt the grim anger spiraling inside himself. "You go back to the house with Joe," he said to the girls. "It's time for me to pay another visit."

He caught Joe's quick nod as the girls took to their horses and followed him out of town. Fargo waited till they were out of sight before he made his way to the white house and saw that the pony rig was not outside.

No one answered his knock on the door, and he withdrew to the old shed to wait. He dismounted, folded himself on the ground, and let time go by. Something between uneasiness and alarm began to stab at him as the day went into afternoon and Doc Elkins still hadn't returned to his office. When the sun began to slide toward the horizon, he climbed onto the Ovaro and rode the road from town. A country doctor often traveled long distances, he knew, and perhaps that was the explanation. But he rode slowly, cautiously, his eyes sweeping the land along the sides of the road.

He had gone perhaps a few miles from town when he spied the pony cart drawn up near a dense stand of box elder, the slender, black-coated figure sitting quietly inside. He felt the frown on his brow as he steered the Ovaro up the slight incline to the cart and reined to a halt.

Doc Elkins looked at him with a smile as tired as his eyes. "Been out here thinking," he said.

"Now you can start answering," Fargo said.

"You found the records," the doctor said.

"Who told you?"

The tired smile widened a fraction. "You didn't close the window tight. I always close windows tight. I knew then you'd come back," Doc Elkins said. "How'd you know I lied about not keeping records?"

"A man who keeps his first stethoscope, his medical books, his first fee, a man with a waiting room all ordered and neat with everything in place, that kind of man keeps records," Fargo said.

The weary smile stayed. "The Trailsman," Doc Elkins said. "Reading trails, just of another kind. I should have expected as much."

"Why'd you lie about the records?" Fargo asked, his tone grown harsh.

"We'll talk, but before we do, give me your gun," the man said.

"Like hell," Fargo snapped.

"There are two big Winchester rifles pointed at you this very moment from inside those trees behind me," Doc Elkins said. Fargo's eyes flicked to the trees, but the lowering dusk let him see only darkness. "Isn't that right, Dermott?" the doctor called.

"Right at his gut," a voice answered from inside the trees.

"Your gun, please," the doctor said, and Fargo swore silently. He was in the clear, a perfect target for even a poor marksman, and he couldn't see anything to fire at. He slowly lifted the Colt from its holster and handed it to the man.

"Now the rifle," Doc Elkins said, and Fargo drew the big Sharps from the saddle holster, slid it at the man.

"You expected the three girls to show up all along, didn't you?" Fargo said.

"No," Doc Elkins said. "No more than Clarence did." Fargo's brows lifted as he waited. "Oh, Clarence told me he'd written to them, kind of a last resort. He didn't want anyone else to get his fortune. He hoped that maybe one of them would get his letter and show up. But he never expected all three would. He wrote to addresses that were decades old. He'd no way of knowing if his letters would reach any of the girls." The doctor uttered a wry sound. "But, amazingly, all three of his letters reached their destination, something Clarence never dreamed would happen."

"That was where things started to get out of hand," Fargo said.

"That's right. No one expected that. I certainly hadn't," Doc Elkins said.

"Who else knew the three daughters existed besides you?" Fargo questioned.

"Nobody. He paid me well to keep his secret all these years," Doc Elkins said. "Their mothers meant nothing to him at the time. They were only a good romp in bed."

"He paid them off, too," Fargo said.

"That's right, agreed to let the girls use his name and made sure the mothers realized they'd never get a cent from him if they ever returned to these parts."

"Why'd he name them all the same?" Fargo asked.

"He liked the name. Clarence did things like that. And maybe in the back of his mind, he wanted to be sure there'd be one Penelope Julia Peabody around someday if he needed her. That was like Clarence, too."

"I know, a careful man, always covering himself," Fargo said as he recalled Joe Plum's words. "Seems you learned from him."

"Meaning what?" Doc Elkins said.

"You knew Clarence Peabody hid his fortune where it'd be damn hard to find," Fargo said, and the man's shrug was an admission. "You sent that letter that brought me here," Fargo said.

"Yes," the doctor said.

"Gordon MacNiff wanted to make sure nobody claimed the estate. He was willing to kill to see to that," Fargo said. "You figured to sit back and wait. If one of the girls did get through, you planned to let me find the fortune for her and then move in."

"Exactly," the doctor said with his weary smile.

"Only that's out now," Fargo said.

"On the contrary. I've merely had to put in a change of plans," the man said, signaled with his hand, and Fargo saw the two men step from the dark of the trees, their rifles trained on him. "You will take me to the fortune directly," Doc Elkins said.

"The girls are expecting me. I don't show, they'll know something's gone wrong," Fargo said.

"They are my prisoners now, along with the old man," Doc Elkins said.

"Good try, but I'm not buying," Fargo said. "Joe would hear anyone coming to the house. They'd never sneak up on him from outside."

"They didn't come from outside. Or I should say she didn't come from outside," the doctor said. "Asa Toomey took the old man at gunpoint, then the girls. They were completely surprised."

"Asa Toomey? How does she figure in this?" Fargo frowned.

"She had a son that was killed working for Clarence Peabody. It was Peabody's fault, but he never did a thing about it. She went to work for him twenty-five years ago, just to wait for a chance to get something out of the tight bastard. The years went by, but she hung in, and when old Clarence jumped into that gorge, we talked. We decided to work together to get hold of the fortune."

"You had to get rid of Mike Shaw so he wouldn't get in the way," Fargo said.

"That's unimportant now," Doc Elkins said. "What's important is that I have the girls and the old man. They're in one of the mine shafts with a stick of dynamite. Asa Toomey will set off the dynamite if she sees anyone come looking. You know how many

134

mine shafts there are. There's no chance you could search them all without being seen."

Fargo swore under his breath as he realized the truth of the man's words. "What now?" he asked.

"You find that fortune Clarence Peabody hid away. You do that, and nothing happens to the girls or Joe Plum. Asa will see they're fed till I get back."

"It's somewhere on Arrow Mountain. That's the heart of Pawnee country. You might never get back," Fargo said.

The doctor's lips pursed in thought before he answered. "A risk I'm prepared to take," he said, and turned to the two men. "Dermott, here, and Crayle will never take their eyes off you. One or both will be watching you at all times. You want Joe Plum and the girls to stay alive, you'd best not try any tricks."

"You could take the money and run with it and forget about Asa Toomey. She'd do them all in then," Fargo said.

"I wouldn't do that. I'd return to give her her share," the man said indignantly.

"An honorable man," Fargo said thinly.

"That's right," Doc Elkins snapped.

"Your own definition," Fargo said, and the man's lips tightened. He snapped the reins over the pony cart and spoke to the two men.

"I'll meet you at the first fork," he said, and sent the cart bouncing down the slope. The man called Dermott, thin and tall, with a pencil-thin mustache, brought his horse up behind him and Fargo saw the length of rope in his hands. He felt Dermott tie his wrists behind him as the other man, Crayle, square-faced and stone-eyed, kept the Winchester trained on him. Finished, Dermott brought his horse alongside him as Crayle swung in on the other side.

"Ride," Dermott said, and started down the slope and onto the road. They moved unhurriedly along the night road and finally halted, drew to one side where the road forked. Doc Elkins came along soon after, riding a big bay gelding.

"We'll camp for the night up a ways," he said. "Come morning, we'll make time."

Fargo rode silently and let his thoughts race. The two men were grim, and he felt one pair of eyes on him at all times. They'd be the greatest problem, he knew. He had to find the right place and the right time, and he had one advantage: they had to let him lead the way. He'd choose his moment. The rest was to make it count. He settled down, let himself relax.

Doc Elkins looked quietly confident and Fargo smiled inwardly. He liked that.

# 6

Morning dawned warm and bright, and Fargo had slept soundly. The two guards watched him as he washed and dressed, took turns as they got themselves ready. Doc Elkins had shed his black frock coat and sat his horse in shirt sleeves and a vest.

"I can't break trail and make time with my hands tied behind me," Fargo said.

"Fair enough," the doctor said. "Just remember that Dermott and Crayle are crack shots."

"Don't doubt it," Fargo said pleasantly as he swung onto the pinto. He set an unhurried pace west and felt the two men's eyes on him as he rode, their rifles held across their laps and ready to fire at an instant.

He set a course that dipped south and turned west again as it crossed into Kansas Territory. By noon he followed the line of the river the French explorers had called the *Marais des Cygnes*, the Marsh of the Swans, and by dusk the Flint Hills Range loomed dead ahead. Arrow Mountain lay in the center of the range, and he called a halt at a circle of hawthorns to camp. He ate the strips of jerky they gave him before they tied him for the night, and he stayed awake as silence settled over the scene.

Doc Elkins had told the truth about his two hired guns. They had never taken their eyes from him, Fargo mused. But the land had been too tame for him to chance anything. The morning would bring a different terrain, but time was beginning to press on him. Another two days would bring them to Arrow Mountain and almost certainly a Pawnee war party. That'd be the end of the search. The only way to find a way through Indian country was for him to go on ahead and use all the trail wisdom he knew. But Elkins would never agree to that. He'd see it only as a trick, a ruse to give him a chance to escape. He had planned everything except the final truth. Nobody could lead the way unscathed through Indian country under guard. Fargo settled himself on the ground, grimly aware that he was running out of time to find that moment he had to have.

He was glad to see a gray sky when morning dawned, and it remained that way as they started to ride west, the hills quickly rising up in front of them. A gust of wind blew a flurry of raindrops that disappeared as quickly as they had come. But the skies stayed leaden as he led the way into the lower hills. Elkins called a halt to let the horses drink of a small stream, and Fargo felt the man's eyes on him.

"You don't figure to search all of Arrow Mountain. You must have something else to go on," Doc Elkins said.

"Somewhere up near the very top," Fargo lied. "But if I were you. I'd have my boys watching for Pawnees instead of keeping their eyes glued on me."

Doc Elkins smiled chidingly. "You'd like that, wouldn't you?" he said.

"Suit yourself. Don't say I didn't warn you," Fargo answered, and turned the Ovaro away from the stream. His eyes swept the foothills as he rode forward, searching the terrain, seeking a place he could use, and cursed silently as nothing revealed itself.

A light rain began to fall and he continued to scan the rocky hills that now rose up on all sides of him. He'd climbed perhaps another hour when he spotted the steep, narrow defile that rose up to the right, and his eyes narrowed as he surveyed the passage. It would have to do, he muttered bitterly to himself, and reined to a halt. Doc Elkins halted beside him.

"This rain's going to get heavier and the footing treacherous. We'll take a shortcut, that pass over there," he said.

Doc Elkins followed his gaze and frowned. "Pretty damn steep," he muttered.

"That's what makes it a shortcut," Fargo said. "The horses can make it. We'll make up half a day by not circling through these foothills."

"All right," the man said, and fell back as Dermott and Crayle drew up behind the Ovaro.

Fargo's eyes were on the narrow defile as he rode slowly toward it, measuring, gauging, planning. Elkins was unaware that the thin, double-edged throwing knife was in the calf holster around his leg, but he'd found no chance to use the blade this far, and he wasn't counting on it now. He'd use the steepness of the defile and the fact that they'd have to go up it single-file. The horses would have a job of it, and he counted on that fact, too. They'd send him up first, Dermott and Crayle close behind him and the doctor

*139*

following last. Fargo scanned the defile again as he neared the start of it and took in the pebbly dirt that formed the floor of the steep passage.

His eyes narrowed as he stared up into the defile. Three-quarters of the way up it grew even steeper. They'd have to go slow, let the horses dig in hard for firm footing. That was the place. That would be the moment, he murmured silently.

Elkins' voice cut into his thoughts as they reached the start of the defile. "Rein up," the man called out.

Fargo turned in the saddle and saw his tired eyes staring up at the steepness of the passage, the rock walls reaching up on both sides of it.

Doc Elkins turned his eyes on the Ovaro before he spoke. "That horse can outclimb any of the others," he said, turned his eyes on Fargo. "Maybe you've ideas of reaching the top first and taking off while we're still fighting our way up."

"Wouldn't think of it," Fargo said.

"I'll make sure of that," the man said. "Dermott and Crayle, you'll lead the way up. You follow Crayle, Fargo. I'll be right behind you."

Fargo kept his face expressionless. "Whatever you like," he said as he raged inwardly. The man's suspicions were wrong, but he had just ruined his plans. Fargo swore silently. He had counted on being first in line up the narrow defile, and when the moment came at the very steepest section, he'd make the Ovaro slip. The horse would crash its rump into Dermott's mount. The man's horse would lose footing immediately, crash back into Crayle, and like dominoes falling, they'd all go down the narrow defile, all three horses falling and riders toppling. Only the Ovaro, first in line, would keep his footing and pull onto the top of the passage and freedom. And now, unwittingly, Elkins had shattered the entire scheme. *Goddamn*, Fargo swore under his breath as Dermott started into the defile, Crayle going in close behind him.

Fargo followed, and Elkins came up behind him. The defile rose sharply at once and he felt the hindquarter muscles of the Ovaro grow tight as the horse dug hooves into the ground. Dermott had the saddle sense not to push his horse, Fargo saw, and set a careful pace up the narrow passage. Throwing a quick glance behind him, he saw Elkins was staying close. But he was riding with only one hand on the reins, the other on the butt of the six-gun at his side. Fargo turned forward and the smile was grim that touched his lips. Elkins would have damn little control of his horse one-handed, he grunted with satisfaction.

The rain continued to fall in a light but steady rate, and Fargo peered up past Crayle and Dermott. The very steep section of the defile was nearing, and his lips became a thin line. He had to act. Another chance might not come along, and his mind tossed thoughts frantically. His original plan was still the only chance he had, but with changes. Only one domino now and the razor-sharp throwing knife still in its calf holster brought into swift and sudden play. On-the-spot adaptations that had to work in split-second tandem. He shifted in the saddle, every muscle taut.

In front of him, Dermott and Crayle had reached the very steep section of the defile, and Fargo saw they had trouble immediately, their mounts fighting for footholds. Dermott slowed again, letting his horse take time to find its footing, and Crayle stayed right behind him. Fargo reached the steep incline and slowed the Ovaro more than he had to as he put more space between himself and Crayle. He felt the doctor's horse at his heels as he almost brought the pinto to a halt.

"Keep moving, dammit," Elkins called out, and Fargo let the Ovaro dig hard into the steep and slippery passage and moved upward. But he held the horse under tight rein, his eyes on Crayle in front of him. Crayle had slowed also, but there was still enough space. Fargo leaned forward in the saddle as his right hand reached down to his calf. He waited a moment longer, measuring the distance to the man in front of him. He felt Elkins pressing close again and let the man come a little closer.

Fargo's hand was on the hilt of the throwing knife in the calf holster when he yanked the reins sharply. The Ovaro half-reared, slid hard backward, his heavy rump smashing into the horse behind him.

"Goddamn," Fargo heard Elkins shout and then the cry of surprise and pain as he was tossed from the saddle and his horse fell onto its haunches.

In front of him, Crayle spun in the saddle, but Fargo had the thin, double-edged throwing knife in his hand. Crayle tried to bring his rifle around as he fought to keep his mount in hand. Fargo threw the knife underhand, and the perfectly balanced blade hurtled up through the rain. It struck before Crayle could bring the rifle around and plunged hilt-deep into the base of the man's throat. Fargo saw Crayle's eyes seem to pop from his head. Blood welled up and burst from the man's mouth as he toppled across the rear of his horse and his rifle fell noisily to the ground.

Fargo was already sliding from the Ovaro, one hand clutched on the reins to hold the pinto in place.

He landed on the ground in the six inches of space between the horse and the wall of the defile as Dermott threw a glance backward. The quick glance told the man enough, and he bent low in the saddle, kept his horse steady, and continued to climb. Fargo peered down the passage. Elkins' big bay had pulled himself up from his haunches and was standing quietly. He found Elkins lying a half-dozen feet farther down the incline. The man lay motionless and Fargo saw the slow stain of red seeping from his head where it lay against a sharp-edged rock at the side of the passage. Doc Elkins had made his last house call.

Fargo turned his gaze up the defile and saw Dermott nearing the top, still bent low in the saddle. The man had acted smartly, no attempt to turn and use his rifle and maybe lose control of his horse. Now he'd hunker down and wait, knowing that his quarry had to move up, had to come out of the defile.

Fargo drew a deep breath and leaned against the stone wall of the passage. There was no need to hurry. Dermott would wait to try to pick him off, confident he had all the advantages. And he did, at the moment, Fargo muttered inwardly. He watched as Crayle's horse, free of rider, slowly pulled himself up and moved onto the top of the passage.

Fargo kept the Ovaro in place as he retrieved the throwing knife, cleaned the blade, and put it back into the calf holster. He squeezed past the pinto as he moved down the passage. He did the same with the doctor's horse and halted over the crumpled form. He reached down, took his Colt back, and stared down at the still form. For a moment he felt something close to sadness.

"Old fool," Fargo murmured. "A doctor's supposed to save lives, not take them."

He turned away abruptly and walked up through the rain. He passed the horses and ran his hands over the Ovaro's neck to keep him calm. The rain continued its steady fall as Fargo leaned against the rock side of the passage. Maybe another two hours before night dropped over the hills, he estimated. It would be a wet wait, but wet was better than dead.

He lowered himself to the ground and rested against the stone wall. The horses had both grown calm, content to stay in place with an occasional snort of air, and Fargo let the time slowly tick away. He was not waiting alone, he was certain. Dermott could do no less. A hired gun would quit and run only if there was nothing left but that. Dermott figured he had a lot left, and by now he'd have settled into the best position to see the mouth of the defile.

Fargo relaxed as the day began to slide toward dusk. The rain began to taper off into intermittent showers. Fargo pushed himself to his feet. By now, Dermott would have realized what he intended to do, and Fargo's eyes fixed at the top of the passage in case the man decided to stop waiting and try to come after him. But nothing moved. It was plain that Dermott was going to play out his hand. Fargo let the dusk drift over the hills until it shredded away into darkness. He began to climb the defile on foot as night embraced the hills. Behind him, he heard the Ovaro start to follow, hooves dislodging small stones as he dug hard into the slippery steepness.

Fargo made no move to stop the horse. Silence wouldn't really matter. Dermott was waiting, peering through the blackness. He'd have to peer real hard,

Fargo reckoned. There was no moon and the clouds were still hanging low across the sky. Fargo continued to climb up the very steep section, slowed as the defile began to level off near the top. He moved a dozen yards farther, and the end of the passage beckoned to him. He dropped to his stomach and began to crawl the last half-dozen yards, paused when he reached the top, and slid sideways to the edge of the rock wall. The moonless night provided only blackness, the rocks beyond nothing but deeper darkness, shadows against shadows. And out there, Dermott waited to kill him. But darkness was impartial, and he knew the man could see no more than he could. He swept the terrain beyond the defile with a slow, peering glance, trying to find a shape, spot a movement, but saw only the blackness. He had to make Dermott show himself, do something to fix his position.

His hand closed around a scattering of small rocks and he drew them in, lifted one arm, and tossed them across to the other side of the mouth of the passage. He had the Colt up, ready to fire, but there was no flash in the dark, nothing to pinpoint Dermott's position. Fargo felt the frown dig into his brow. It had been an old trick and perhaps Dermott just didn't bite. Or he wasn't out there in the blackness. Fargo shook away the thought. If he were wrong, it'd be his last mistake.

He turned at the sound behind him and saw the Ovaro appear. He pushed himself to his feet, grabbed the horse by the cheek strap, and pulled him to the stone side of the defile. The big bay came along a few moments later, slowed, and Fargo moved around behind his horse, caught hold of the bay's reins. He held them for a moment as he crept forward alongside the horse, brought the Colt up, and slammed his hand down hard on the bay's rump. The horse bolted forward out of the defile, racing as though a rider were atop its back trying to get away.

Fargo saw the yellow flashes first as the shots exploded out of the blackness—one, two, three, two more as Dermott fired at the horse that raced through the night. Fargo aimed into the dark and waited for another flash of gunfire. It came a split second later, and he fired, moving the Colt a fraction of an inch to either side with each shot. He heard the guttural cry of pain. He waited, listened, and the groans drifted through the blackness, unmistakable, to finally die away. There was only silence now, but he stayed motionless, caution as much a part of him as his skin. The pale shaft of light came down with suddenness as the clouds broke and a line of low boulders took shape, beyond them the tall peaks of the mountain range.

Fargo rose, moved forward, and spotted the arm hanging half over the top of one of the rocks. Three long strides brought him to the place, and he saw Dermott, facedown on the ground, a small red rivulet seeping from two places in his body, one just under the neck, the other where a bullet had emerged through his shoulder blade. Fargo stepped back, holstered the Colt, and walked to where the pinto waited. He climbed onto the horse and rode on along the rock-bound passages. He found one that led downward and followed it until he reached a flat ledge where a blue spruce spread its branches. He dismounted, set down his bedroll, and stretched out in the night. Only one part of it had come to an end.

There was too much still to come. He closed his eyes and drew sleep around him as a welcome cloak.

The morning sun woke him with its warm caress, and he found a mountain stream that let him wash, water the pinto, and refill his canteen. He continued on down the mountainside when he took to the saddle and sent the horse eastward. He didn't halt till the day came to an end, then he camped, slept again, and let himself wake with the dawn. He rode hard and crossed into Missouri a little after the noon hour. He had reached the hills surrounding the mine as the afternoon began to fade, and he sent the horse upward to circle around along the back of the mine and emerged at a spot that let him scan the hillside of mine shafts and the house below.

He slid from the saddle, put the horse behind a tall, flat-sided boulder, and dropped to one knee. He moved his gaze from one mine-shaft entrance to another and back again, but he saw nothing to help him pick out the right shaft. His attention went to the big house. A wisp of smoke drifted from the chimney, and as he watched, the front door opened and Asa Toomey stepped out, a broom in hand, and swept the front steps clean. The very act seemed to mock reality. The time for sweeping and cleaning and housekeeping was finished. But the habits of a lifetime stayed on. He watched her finish and go back inside the house as twilight began to drift into the hollow of land below.

He settled down against the tall rock to let night blanket the land. But the blanket came with a pale-silver light, and he had to expect that Asa Toomey sat at a window of the house, waiting and watching, her eyes on the hillside. She'd be able to see him in the moonlight as he crossed the smooth hillside and made his way from shaft to shaft. He recalled Elkins' threat. They had obviously rigged up a long wire to a detonator in the house. But the woman had to sleep sometime. Fargo frowned. She couldn't stay awake and on watch day and night. Perhaps she went to sleep in the mornings on the reasonable assumption he wouldn't come in broad daylight. Perhaps, he grunted with grimness. If he were wrong, she'd certainly see him. If she slept by night, perhaps he could circle around to the back of the house, slip inside, and take her by surprise. If, he grunted with added grimness. It was all too great a risk. It'd take but an instant for Asa Toomey to set off the detonator and blow away four lives.

He settled back against the rock as he discarded the thoughts. He'd wait, get some sleep himself. It had been a hard day's ride. He'd wait for daylight and Asa Toomey to leave the house, and come out into the open, too far away to reach any detonator. He closed his eyes, made himself as comfortable as he could, and slept quickly. The night had enough hours left in it to allow a good, sound sleep, and he woke with the warmth of the morning sun quickly beginning to bake the rock at his back.

His eyes went to the house at once. It was still. He rose, backed to where the Ovaro waited out of sight, and used his canteen to freshen up and soothe the dryness in his throat. He drew the big Sharps from the rifle case beside the saddle and returned to his vantage point. The house remained still for another hour, until the tiny spiral of smoke began to drift from the chimney again. Asa Toomey was awake, he grunted. She wasn't sleeping by day. He waited, and finally the door opened and the woman came out, a wooden bucket in one hand, a sack of something in the other. Soup and bread, Fargo guessed, and he watched as Asa Toomey slowly made her way up the hillside. He watched her as she moved toward a shaft entrance at the other end of the hill, high above but almost directly in line with the house. He smiled thinly. It was the best shaft from which to run the detonator wire to the house.

Asa climbed slowly and went into the shaft. Fargo waited, brought the rifle up, and finally the woman reappeared, the sack empty and draped across the bucket. She started directly down the hillside, and Fargo rose, aimed, and fired. The shot sent a spray of dirt up in front of Asa Toomey's feet, and she halted in surprise and peered across the hillside. He stepped into the open and started toward her when she dropped the bucket and began to run downhill toward the house.

"Dammit," Fargo spit out as he brought the rifle up and fired again. This time the shot passed through the billowing folds of her gray housedress. "Don't be a damn fool," Fargo shouted, and the woman came to a halt, her face set and her eyes narrowed as he reached her. "It's over," Fargo said.

"Where's Elkins?" Asa Toomey asked.

"Dead," Fargo answered, and her expression didn't change. "You can believe me."

"I suppose so," she muttered. "Else you wouldn't be here."

"Where's the detonator?" he asked.

"Living room, by the window," the woman said.

He gestured with the rifle. "Ladies first."

She turned and walked ahead of him down the hillside. He could feel the simmering anger inside her. They had almost reached the house when he called a halt.

"Lay down," he said, and with a stony glare she obeyed. "Stay there till I come out," he warned her. "Don't be stupid about anything."

She said nothing, and he hurried into the house and saw the detonator at once where Asa Toomey had said it was. A Winchester rested upright beside it. He stepped to the device and with a quick motion yanked the wire out and stepped back. He took up the Winchester, emptied the shells from it, and picked up the detonator box. Asa Toomey hadn't moved, he saw as he stepped from the house.

"You can get up," he said as he set the device on the ground and brought his boot smashing down on it with all his weight and strength. The box shattered into useless bits and pieces and he met Asa Toomey's unflinching, cold-anger stare.

"You can start packing up," he said. "Or did you do that already?"

"Some," she muttered.

"Finish," he said, and his eyes were on Asa Toomey as she turned away. He felt the frown touch his brow and the sudden jab of uneasiness inside his gut. There'd been more than anger in Asa Toomey's eyes as she turned from him. Not defeat, not the resignation of losing, not even bitterness. There'd been a flash of something close to triumph, an instant of smugness. Something was wrong, he murmured inside himself.

"Hold on," he called out, and the woman stopped, her expressionless face turning to look at him. "Lead the way to the shaft."

Asa Toomey's eyes darkened. "You know which one they're in. You watched me go to it," she said.

"I want company," he said.

"This is nothing but damn-fool nonsense," she snapped.

"Start walking," Fargo ordered, and fell back of the woman as she began to trudge up the hillside.

She walked with her expressionless face set tightly. They were halfway to the mine shaft when she glared back at him. "What's the point of this?" she snapped.

"I'm not sure," Fargo said evenly.

"You some kind of crazy man?" Asa Toomey threw back.

"Might be," Fargo said. "Keep walking."

Asa Toomey turned away and pulled herself up the hillside, and he stayed close behind her. The entrance to the mine shaft loomed up in front of him, only a few dozen yards away now. He saw Asa Toomey lick lips that were not only thin but suddenly dry. She halted again, threw him a sidelong glance. "Think you can find your way from here?" she said.

"No," Fargo answered. "Keep walking, all the way into the shaft." He saw the woman's face grow tighter, and there was nervousness in the glare she threw at him. She approached the entranceway of the mine shaft and halted again. He came up beside her, his hand closing around her elbow.

"We'll go in together," he said, and felt her body pull back. He started forward, pulling her along with him.

"No," she whispered. "No."

He didn't stop pulling her with him. "You afraid of the dark?" he muttered.

Suddenly with a cry of frustration and fear mixed

together, she tore her arm from his grasp and shrank away. She stared at him and her breath came in quick, dry gasps.

"There's a triphammer wire, isn't there?" Fargo rasped.

Asa Toomey nodded, the fear still in her face.

"Where?" he snapped.

"A half-dozen feet on. You wouldn't see it if you didn't know it was there," she said.

"High enough to set off and low enough for you to step over when you brought the food," he finished, and her silence was finally made of defeat, only a dullness left in her eyes. He moved carefully forward and spied the thin strip of wire in the half-light inside the shaft, followed the one end to the stick of dynamite and the triphammer poised to smash down on it and send it exploding. Even a poor explosion would send the shored-up walls of the shaft crashing down to bury anyone inside it. Carefully, he took the wire from around the triphammer, pulled the stick of dynamite free, and pushed it into his pocket.

He turned to glance at Asa Toomey. She stood quietly, but now her shoulders hung low, her body seemed to sag into itself.

"Damn his soul," she murmured, and Fargo had no need to ask who she meant. "He always wins, always gets his way, even now."

Fargo waited as she moved slowly out of the entrance to the mine shaft to trudge down the hillside.

The Trailsman spun, strode forward deeper into the shaft. The light was almost at an end when he came upon the four figures bound and gagged on the floor of the shaft. He freed them quickly—Joe Plum first, and the man helped untie the girls with him.

"Jesus, if you aren't a wonderful sight to see," Joe said. "What in hell happened? We know Doc Elkins was part of it."

"He figured to make me into his personal guide to fame and fortune," Fargo said. "His last mistake."

He felt Penny's hand on his arm, and Penelope and Pepper were beside her at once, all crowding around him.

Penny reached up, her lips brushing his cheek. "We're running out of ways to say thank you," she said.

"Will you still go on with us?" Penelope asked.

"Have to," Fargo said blandly, and drew a trio of frowns. "You three owe me a thousand dollars plus a five-hundred-dollar bonus. I figure the only way I'm going to get paid is if I get that money."

"Yes, that's for sure," Penny said.

"Besides, I always finish what I start," Fargo added. "Now, let's go down and get you all packed for travel."

"After we take a bath," Pepper said to a chorus of agreement.

Joe Plum walked beside Fargo as he followed the three young women down the hillside.

"You can get off here, Joe," Fargo said. "You've done your part of it, and I can pay you now. You were a real help."

"Going into Pawnee country you'll be needing all the help you can get," the old miner said.

"You're putting your neck on the line," Fargo reminded him.

"It's an old neck. It's seen enough good times and

bad. Besides, I'm sort of like you. I like to finish a job," Joe said.

Fargo nodded. "We'll sure try," he said.

When they reached the bottom of the hollow, he saw Asa Toomey drive from behind the barn in a battered buckboard, two satchels in the back of it. She went on, not looking at anyone, and disappeared down the road at the other end of the hollow. He waited for the girls to clean and change clothes before he used the outside stall shower beside the house. Pepper was the first to emerge in a fresh yellow shirt with a black riding skirt, and she watched as he dried himself behind the stall.

"Where are the others?" he asked.

"Getting ready," she said.

"Pack only a few things, as little as possible. You want to be able to move fast if you have to. Tell the others," he said, and she disappeared into the house.

The sun had crossed the noon sky when everyone was ready to move, and Fargo led the little troupe out of the hollow, turned west once again, and followed much the same route he'd taken with Elkins. He made camp when night fell and saw the three young women were happy to fall asleep at once. He slept nearby. There was no need for precautions yet.

In the morning they breakfasted on a stand of wild cherry and biscuits Penelope had packed. They rode in a tight group as Fargo set a steady pace that brought them into Kansas Territory and into the Flint Hills by nightfall. Joe made a small fire, and they ate warmed beef jerky.

"Do you think there's a chance of finding it, Fargo?" Penelope asked.

"Wouldn't be here otherwise," Fargo said, and her lips thinned.

"That was a fool question, I guess," she said. "It's just that I'm suddenly afraid."

"Stay that way," Fargo said. "Then you won't do anything dumb." Fargo took the slip of paper from his pocket and stared at it again. "*Kawaharu*," he read aloud. "He wrote it down as the key to all of it."

"But I don't understand what he meant by it," Penny said. "You said the word meant the presence of the great spirit, something sacred."

"There has to be a connection," Fargo said. "We've just got to find it."

"He was a very strange man, it seems," Penelope ventured.

"Yes, and I'm sorry I never knew him," Penny said. "I guess we all feel that way."

"I think I'd have hated him and loved him all at the same time," Pepper remarked thoughtfully.

"You'll have plenty of time for stray thoughts when it's over. Now get some sleep," Fargo said, and Joe stamped out the fire as the night grew still.

Fargo slept quickly and was the first awake when morning came. When the others were ready to move, he took them up into the foothills and beyond. Climbing up to the main body of the range, they turned directly north. He slowed the pace as the afternoon grew long. He had seen the signs but kept the fact to himself, pieces of torn wrist gauntlet, a single trail of unshod ponies, the imprint of moccasins around a campsite. He made camp under a stand of mountain ash, where hills rose up on three sides.

"No fires from now on," he said. "Two of you sleep on that side, one across the camp."

"I'll take the edge over there," Joe Plum said.

Fargo felt Pepper's eyes on him. "Where will you be?" she asked.

He nodded to the slope behind the trees. "Up there," he said.

"Why all this?" Penelope asked.

"A Pawnee scouting party could be riding at dawn. They could easily miss spotting a single form asleep. They wouldn't miss five people grouped together," Fargo said as he rose and took his bedroll from the Ovaro.

He positioned the horses singly in the thick of the trees and climbed up the slope until he found a high place that flattened out under a high-boughed spruce. The night was warm, and he undressed, put his gun belt at his side, and lay down on the bedroll. They'd make Arrow Mountain by the time the next day ended, and he let plans take shape in his mind. "Plans" was perhaps not the right word, he snorted wryly. "Emergency contingencies" was more accurate. He lay quietly as his thoughts idled when he heard the sound in the night and his hand closed around the Colt. He lay still, brought the gun around, and listened. The sound came again, soft footsteps moving through the low brush, climbing toward him.

"Fargo," he heard the half-whispered call and relaxed his finger on the trigger.

"Over here," he said, sat up, and watched the shape materialize under the pale moonlight that filtered though the trees. The shape neared and he saw the slender form, the brown robe wrapped around it, and Pepper halted before him. The bedroll had slipped down to where it barely covered his groin, and he saw her gaze take in his muscled nakedness.

"You're not supposed to be roaming around in the night," he commented.

"I couldn't sleep," she said, and sank down on both knees beside him, her eyes still moving across the beauty of his body.

"Is that all?" he questioned quietly.

"No," she said, and pulled her eyes up to meet his. "The other day Penny said we'd run out of ways to thank you. I haven't," she said. "Surprised?"

"Some," he admitted. "Only grateful doesn't do it, honey."

"What does?"

"Wanting," he said.

She stared into the night for a moment. "That night when you asked if I were really on my way to see you?" she recalled.

"You were very definite about saying no. You telling me now that was a lie?" Fargo queried.

"No, it was the truth. I was on my way to the kitchen for water. But I'd been thinking about you, wondering what it'd be like if I did come visit you," she said. "But I would never have, not then."

"And now?"

"Things are different now," she said. "You know that."

"They are," he agreed.

"One thing more. Maybe it's wrong, but I can't help it. I've been feeling jealous of Penny and Penelope, cheated, like they've had something I should have," she said. "Can you understand that?"

"I think so, but that doesn't matter. What matters is that you feel that way," Fargo answered. "Nothing else."

He reached out, put a hand on her shoulder,

moved, and the robe opened, came away in his hand. She wore nothing beneath, and the longish breasts rose up, beckoned to him. She pushed the robe from her entirely, and he surveyed her, breasts long, filling out at the undersides, smooth with pink-tipped nipples on wide pink circles. Her ribs showed and her waist was very slender, curved into narrow hips where a flat belly slid under a V-shaped dark path that seemed neat enough to have been trimmed. Lean legs, a little thin, seemed longer than they were, with a tensile strength in their loveliness.

She came forward and her arms encircled his shoulders, her breasts smooth against him, the tiny tips instantly firm. He felt the tightness in her, the fiery strength as her mouth opened on his, hungering, taking him in with her tongue. He was erect almost at once as her steel-wire wanting transmitted itself to him with a burning fervor. Her flat belly came hard against him, and Pepper cried out with delight as his thick, pulsating organ pushed against her. She rolled back and forth on him, gasping in delight at touch, sense, feel, and when he turned with her, pressed her onto her back, the slender legs came up at once, clasped around him, squeezed, and fell away. His mouth found the longish breasts, pulled on them, took them deep into him, and she cried out. Her neat little dark patch lifted to rub back and forth against him.

There was no shaking to her, no quivering, yet she seemed alive with a tingling of flesh, a hotness to her skin, and a demand that needed no words. She drew the lean legs up again, rubbed them down along the sides of his body, against his hips, circled his rear with a quick grasp, and released him at once.

"Take me," he heard her whisper. "Take me, Fargo."

Her hands ran up and down his back, pressed into the hollow at the base of his spine, and her hips moved from side to side as she rubbed herself against him. He felt the warm moistness of her against his skin as she opened her long legs, the flesh calling, making its own soundless words of touch. He rose, moved, slid forward, and her wetness embraced him, liquid of liquids, warm wellspring of ecstasy, and he heard his own groan of pleasure as he slid into her.

She moved at once with him, and the tingling of her body against his was a flame of flesh, spurring, urging, compelling. He heard her gasped whispers as she pushed and thrust with him, her body clinging to his as if welded there.

"Ah . . . ah, beautiful . . . beautiful," Pepper murmured. "More, oh, more, never stop, never."

She stayed tight against him, rolled over with him, pushed onto her knees atop him, and drove herself onto him, hard, harder, plunging her breasts against his open lips. She pumped frantically and suddenly she pulled at him, rolled with her arms locked around his back, and he was atop her again as she stiffened, the slender legs clasping hard behind him, holding him deep inside her.

"Oh, now, now . . ." she cried, and he came with her, exploding with her feverish cries, feeling her hands digging into his back. She held hard against him even as the ecstasy exploded away, became the too-quick emptying of all pleasure.

"Oh, my God," she sighed as she lay still against him. "So wonderful, so really wonderful." Her skin stayed hot, he felt, and her hand came down to curl around him, hold with firm tenderness.

"Pepper," he said. "I picked the right name for you."

"Maybe I'll keep it, as a nickname," she said. "I kind of like it."

"Feel better? About everything?" he asked, and she nodded as she lay back, her sigh made of contentment.

"I hate to go back," she said.

"But you will, right now. I need some sleep and so do you, and we'll get damn little of it if you stay. Each day will be hard from now on, every moment made of danger. I want everybody alert and awake."

She nodded reluctantly, rose, and stretched her lean loveliness. He rose as she pulled the robe on. He went halfway down the slope with her, waited till he was sure she had reached the trees below, then he returned to his bedroll.

He hadn't exaggerated any in what he'd told her. Every day, every hour, every minute that lay ahead could be their last. He closed his eyes and let the single word swim through his mind. *Kahawaru.* Pawnee for sacred, the presence of the great spirit, the god of gods. The word was the key, but he had to find the lock. Damn Clarence Peabody and his games and eccentricities, Fargo swore, pushed away further thoughts, and embraced sleep.

# 7

"Three things," he said as they prepared to ride in the morning sun. "Follow orders, no talking, and no lagging behind." He received nods from everyone as the hard set of his jaw emphasized his words.

He turned the Ovaro northward and began to move into Arrow Mountain as the terrain grew green and lush, covered with thick brush and tree growth, lots of hawthorn, red oak, silver maple, and enough evergreens to keep the mountain green through the winter.

He rode point, stayed a good dozen yards ahead of the others. Pepper was next in line and Joe Plum brought up the rear. His eyes ceaselessly swept the land on all sides as he rode, keeping a slow, steady pace. He made a wide circle to avoid a Pawnee hunting party hauling a slain moose. The constant vigilance, tension an invisible companion in the saddle, sapped the strength more than a day's hard riding, and when dusk filtered through the trees, he made camp under a wide, rock ledge and saw fatigue on every face.

They ate with a minimum of conversation, and he let the others fall asleep before he took his bedroll from beneath the ledge and set it down higher up under the drooping branches of a bitternut. He slept quickly but woke twice to the sounds of moose moving through the hills and the odor of bear prowling more than close enough. When dawn came, he was back under the rock ledge. He found a small stream that let everyone wash and soon led the single-file line deeper into the mountain. He stayed in thick tree cover, rode through the speckled yellow of the sun as it fought its way through the leaves. They were moving steadily upward, but the mountain allowed for a slow, circling pattern that avoided sharp inclines. Arrow Mountain, it was called, but compared to the great ranges of the Rockies, it was more of a large hill. He followed a path through thick red oaks and raised his hand suddenly as he saw the marks on the ground. He stared at the trail signs as the others slowly came up.

"There's a real big Pawnee camp up here." He frowned.

"How do you know that?" Penny asked.

"That hunting party dragged their moose and three more kills through here. Not more than a few hours ago. That's too much meat for them, even for a large war party. That's food for a full-size camp," Fargo said. His eyes moved along the marks on the ground. They would be easy to follow. "Let's go see," he said. "Single-file, slow and careful."

He led the way along the trail, perhaps another mile through the lush mountainside, when his nostrils picked up the camp long before it came into sight. He halted, drew in the scent of meat being smoked, hides drying, freshly skinned kills, that special mixture of blood and entrails and woodsmoke. He gestured to the others behind him. They dismounted with him, followed as he moved forward on foot up a shallow slope thick with hawthorns. The top of the slope looked down at a large, cleared area that was the Pawnee camp. He counted at least ten tepees, meat-drying racks, a row of hot stones with stone vessels boiling atop them, forty to fifty braves, and plenty of squaws, some pounding hides, others gathering bundles of twigs. It was a busy place.

His eyes narrowed as he scanned the camp again.

"Number-one camp?" Joe muttered beside him.

Fargo didn't answer for a moment. The Pawnee had no sentries, he noted. They felt absolutely secure. But there was something more, and he nodded toward the right side of the campsite. Three medicine men stood apart from the rest of the camp, the robes of their full, priestly regalia folded on the ground in front of them, their medicine bundles placed atop each robe.

"Even a big camp usually has only one shaman," Fargo said. "There must be something special about this place."

His glance went to a half-dozen squaws as they loaded bundles of twigs onto three travois, and he watched them move single-file out of the far end of the camp. They went into the trees, and the movement of branches traced their path up a long slope.

"I want to see where they're going," Fargo muttered. "Stay behind me."

"Why?" Penelope asked.

"Something's going on. Twig bundles like that are often used for ritual fire," he said.

He moved backward, keeping in the trees, and paralleled the path of the three squaws as they dragged their travois upward. He stayed a little behind and far to the right of them until the ground began to level. He turned in, moved closer to the squaws, and suddenly the very flat, round stone plateau appeared before him. The squaws came into direct sight as they moved onto the open, flat circle of stone. Fargo crept closer, dropped to one knee as he drew near enough to see properly.

The flat circle held two tall totem poles and one stone carving of a deer. Three Pawnee braves stood guard around the perimeter of the flat circle, each with a bow slung across his back and a lance in his hand. As Fargo watched, the squaws placed the bundles of twigs in front of the totem poles and the stone carving, quickly withdrew and started back down the hill.

"There's going to be a ritual tonight," Fargo whispered. "An important one."

"There's going to be a full moon tonight, too," Joe Plum said.

"That fits perfectly," Fargo said.

"That explains the three shamans," Joe commented.

"Partly. I'd guess they're permanent here," Fargo said. "This is a sacred place. That's why the stone carving and those two totems and the three guards. No one dares come here except at certain times, and then only in the presence of the shamans. Those three guards have been cleansed by the shamans so they can stay here. Any other tribal member caught up here without a shaman's approval would be killed. So you can figure what they'd do to an outsider that violated the sacred place."

"I don't want to think about it," Pepper whispered. "Let's get out of here."

"Stay put," Fargo hissed, and fell silent as he slowly scanned the perimeter of the flat circle.

Most of the wall that surrounded the area was solid stone that rose up vertically. But he spied four places where the solidity of the wall was fissured, two with rocks protruding and two where hardy mountain shrub pushed out from the stone. His eyes grew narrow as he slowly swept the area again, and the thoughts that tumbled through his mind tantalized, mocked reason even as they invited acceptance. He gestured to the others and backed away, stayed on the level land as he melted deep into the hawthorns before he called a halt and sank down to the ground.

"Why aren't we going on?" Penny asked.

"Because we'll stay here till dark and then go back. I want to see what goes on tonight," Fargo said.

"Why?" Penelope asked.

"Had a thought," he answered. "Too crazy to accept, too crazy to reject." He leaned his head back against a tree trunk as the others settled down. "If you wanted to hide a fortune, what kind of place would you pick?" he asked almost casually.

"Someplace nobody would think of looking," Penny answered.

"Or someplace where they could never get to it if they did find out where," Fargo said, watching the little frowns touch each girl's brow as his words danced in their heads. "A place is sacred because it is the place where the presence of the great spirit appears. That's why it cannot be violated and only the shaman can bring one there."

*"Kawaharu,"* Pepper whispered as she stared wide-eyed at him.

"Go to the head of the class," Fargo said. "Sacred, or a sacred place, or the presence of the great spirit at that place. Pawnee is not an exact language."

"You think the fortune's hidden there?" Penelope asked. "But he couldn't have. How could he do it? How could anyone do it without getting killed?"

"Haven't figured that part out yet," Fargo admitted.

"You've got to be wrong. It'd be impossible," Penelope said.

"He did stash it away over the years, Fargo," Joe Plum put in. "He had to have made a lot of trips."

"He'd have been caught at one of them if it were here," Penny said.

"It'd seem that way," Fargo admitted again.

"But you're not convinced," Pepper said.

Fargo drew the slip of paper from his pocket and held it up. "He wrote the word down for you. *Kawaharu* . . . Arrow Mountain. That's where we are. It fits, crazy or not. Maybe the rest will before the night's over."

"And if it doesn't?" Pepper asked.

"We try to get away from here with our scalps still on," Fargo answered, then leaned back and closed his eyes. "Now I'm going to nap," he muttered.

He listened to the others settle down, and only the calls of mountain birds broke the silence. He dozed, woke when he felt the sun leave. He rose to his feet as night came swiftly to wrap the mountain in darkness. But a full moon rose almost as quickly and insinuated its pale light through the leaves.

"Let's go," Fargo said. "I don't want to miss any of the show."

He moved through the darkness and the others followed, slowing as the flickering light appeared in the distance. He went on, in a half-crouch, following the light, which grew stronger, and soon the flat circle appeared. The twig bundles had been set afire and they burned in front of the three sacred objects. Fargo settled down on one knee and felt Pepper against him at one side, Penny's thigh touching his at the other. Joe Plum and Penelope had dropped to their stomachs as they peered through the brush. He heard the chanting first, and his eyes were on the pathway that the squaws had used. The chanting grew stronger, and soon the first figure to appear onto the flat circle of stone was one of the shamans. He was clothed in a robe that reached the ground, his medicine bundle in one hand, his neck adorned with various claws, stones, feathers, and beads.

A dozen squaws came next, each bearing a stone vessel filled with liquid. They placed the vessels in front of the totems and the stone carving and withdrew quickly. They stood aside as the line of braves came from the pathway onto the flat circle. Three drummers and the other two shamans brought up the rear of the procession. The squaws backed farther and silently went down the pathway as the others gathered themselves in groups in front of the totems and the carving. A shaman led each group as they began to chant and a young boy passed the vessels of liquid from man to man.

The chanting quickly grew stronger and dancing began, individual dances around each totem. More vessels of liquid were passed, and more chanting and dancing began. The initial ordered steps quickly grew erratic, completely individual as each dancer went off on his own. Some halted to lift their arms skyward and cry out hoarsely into the night.

Fargo felt Pepper nudge him as he watched two braves drinking from one of the stone urns. "They're having fits," she said. "What are they drinking?"

"Probably monkshood, jimsonweed, mandrake, belladonna, maybe some wild lettuce and lady's slipper," he told her. "They usually mix up different things."

Wild shouts from the stone circle interrupted him, and he watched a half-dozen braves fling themselves into stiff-bodied, completely uncontrolled dances. They lasted but a few minutes, and when they were over, the dancers collapsed, twitched on the stone, and lay still. The flat circle had become a place of wild shouts and moaned chants and leaping dancers, and the shamans drank from the small urns now, he saw, drawing in long gulps of the liquid. He watched as one took a few minutes to sink to his knees, sway for perhaps ten minutes, and then quietly collapse.

He guessed they had watched for over two hours before the flat circle was silent, covered with bodies that lay partly over each other, some draped against the totems, others simply collapsed into their own little places. But all were drugged, totally and thoroughly unconscious.

"That's it, dammit," Fargo said, and heard the awe in his voice. "Somehow, your pa learned about this wild ritual. They must hold it on the first night of the full moon every month. He came, waited, watched, just as we have, and when they passed out, as they have now, he stashed away another deposit and hightailed it before they woke up. He made them the best damn guardians of his money anybody ever had."

"I'll be dammed," Joe Plum said. "He figured that when the time came, he could take it back the same way."

"Right," Fargo said.

"But where is it?" Pepper frowned.

Fargo pulled himself to his feet. "Someplace out there. We've got maybe an hour or two to find out. I don't know how strong that stuff they drank was," he said, and started forward in a run. He burst onto the flat circle, the others close behind him. "You start at this end of the stone wall around this place," he said to Penelope. "You start at the other end, Penny. Work your way slowly around the circle as you press your hands against the stone. Yell if any section moves or seems loose."

He motioned to Penelope and Joe, and they followed him to the first fissure in the stone where two boulders protruded.

"Push hard," he said as he put his shoulders to the first boulder. It didn't budge and he tried the second. That, too, stayed unmovable.

"There are two more over there," Joe said, and pointed to the next split in the stone wall. Fargo stepped over bodies that breathed with the heavy, deep drafts of the drugged, leaned one hand on the first boulder, and pushed. It didn't budge.

"Wait, we didn't get our shoulders to it," Joe said.

"We're wasting time. Clarence came up here alone. It had to be something he could move by himself," Fargo said. "Let's try those growths of mountain brush.

He skirted more Pawnee bodies as Joe and Penelope hurried after him. He reached the brush and began to push through the strong, wiry stems. Joe and Penelope took another of the bushy growths and did the same. Cursing under his breath, Fargo broke off pieces of stem as he pushed to the very end of the brush, and he stared at roots that grew out of narrow crevices in the stone, everything far too small except for the hardiness of mountain brush.

"Shit," he muttered, and turned as Pepper and Penny drew near, their hands pressed against the vertical stone wall as it circled back onto itself. They halted, finally, in front of him.

"Solid stone," Pepper said.

"Goddamn, it has to be here," Fargo said. "*Kawaharu*. It's the only place that makes any sense. I'm going around this wall again. Maybe you girls didn't press hard enough."

"I'll take the other end," Joe said, and Fargo pushed his palms against the stone, began the slow circle against the flat, vertical wall. He kept pressure against the stone as he moved, used his body and his hands, but he found only solid stone. It was slow, consuming precious time, but he stayed at it and finally met Joe as he finished his half of the wall.

"Nothing," the old miner said balefully. "Completely solid."

"Dammit to hell," Fargo swore as he pounded the side of his fist against the stone in sheer frustration. "It's here, dammit. It has to be. This is the only thing that makes sense."

"What you said seemed to fit, but maybe it doesn't," Penny offered.

"You and your letters seemed to be fakes, but you weren't," he tossed back, and there was apology in her little half-shrug. His eyes swept the area again, danced across the little circle of drugged forms.

"Close by, someplace he could get to quickly, handle alone, and get the hell away fast," Fargo muttered as he thought aloud. A moan cut into his thoughts and he spun around to see one of the three figures sprawled at the base of the stone deer lift its head.

"Goddammit, they're starting to come around," Fargo swore. The Pawnee moaned again and his head came up. He pulled himself to his knees, rose to his feet, and swayed as he worked on getting his eyes uncrossed. Fargo took a long stride forward, brought the butt of the Colt down on the Indian's head.

"This one's on me," he commented.

The Pawnee fell backward, hit against the side of the stone carving, and slid to the ground. But Fargo's eyes held on the stone deer. It had shuddered when the Indian fell against it. He felt his breath draw in sharply as he ran forward, bent low, and pushed his shoulder against the base of the carving. The piece moved, slid sideways on the ground, and he pushed it again. The carving moved farther, and Fargo stared at the long, narrow rectangle in the ground that the base of the carving had covered.

The small cache of sacks stared up at him, and he heard the collective gasp as Penny and the others ran up to him.

"My God, that's it," Penny exclaimed. "You found it."

"He found it," Fargo said of the Pawnee on the ground.

He reached down, pulled up one of the sacks, and found it easy to lift. Each girl could carry two with no problem, and strings around the neck of each sack were long enough to tie together. He felt the coins inside the sacks as he tied them together.

"A tidy sum, I'd guess," he said, and Pepper beamed at him. "Grab a sack. Get them out of there," Fargo ordered, and stepped back.

There were fifteen sacks in all as it turned out, and Joe took an extra load to carry, as did Penny. Pepper paused to watch him push the stone carving back in place.

"Why bother? What difference does it make now?" she asked.

"They wake up, they won't know anyone's been here. We leave that carving out of place and they'll come after us like avenging angels," he told her. "We've two days before we get down from this mountain."

A moan rose, two more following, and Fargo glanced across the circle to see three Pawnee half-turning, beginning to sit up.

"Let's get the hell out of here," Fargo said, and started forward. But he had taken only a half-dozen steps when the night exploded, no moaned sounds this time but shouts of fury and alarm, and he heard the thunder of hooves at the bottom of the path that led to the sacred place. He spun and swept the bodies on the ground with a quick glance, cursed as he counted.

"Forty," he said. "A dozen or so stayed in camp, goddammit, And somebody came onto our horses." He handed the two sacks he carried to Pepper. "Run, get into the hawthorns. I'll be along in a minute."

Spinning, he raced back across the stone circle, swept past the first shaman, scooped up the medicine bundle, did the same with the other two, and drove his long legs for the trees. He plunged into the hawthorns, spotted the others moving ahead of them, and caught up to Pepper first.

"Keep going," he said as he passed her and moved by the others. He continued on into the depths of the trees, pushed his way through the dense underbrush until he halted, turned, and dropped to one knee.

"Everybody down," he said as he drew the big Colt and put the medicine bundles on the ground in front of him. He heard the sound of the horses as they started into the trees and saw Joe push himself behind a tree trunk, six-gun in hand.

"They're crazy mad," Fargo said. "They'll charge in at us and get their ponies bogged down in this thick underbrush. They'll slow and we shoot as soon as they do."

Joe nodded and Fargo's glance went to the three girls. They were flattened onto their stomachs and he nodded in approval. The dark shapes materialized quickly, horses crashing forward and slowing as the underbrush caught at their legs. Fargo counted ten riders, six in one group, four in another. He heard their grunts of command as they made their horses fight their way through the brush. He let them come closer, held his fire for another long minute, and then the Colt exploded in a fusillade of shots. Two of the first group toppled at once, and he saw two more go down as Joe backed up his volley. The others became diving forms as they leapt from their horses, and he saw Joe bring down another.

Fargo reloaded, his eyes straining as he peered through the trees. He made a quick, darting move to another tree as he spotted a Pawnee circling to come in closer. He cast another glance at the brave, let him keep circling, and his eyes were turned away, waiting as the second form came out of the brush in front of him, hurtled forward with a hunting knife in hand. Fargo fired, a single shot that caught the Pawnee full in the chest, and the charging figure stopped as though he'd run into an invisible wall. He had started to collapse when Fargo spun, dropped low, and felt the arrow smash into the tree trunk inches from his head as the Pawnee that had circled came up firing at a run. Fargo got off a shot that missed as the Indian darted sideways, another arrow already on his bowstring. Fargo stayed down, rolled to his right, and the arrow grazed his back. He rolled again, glimpsed the Pawnee standing up now, bowstring drawn back to fire again. But the Indian delayed his shot, tried to take aim, and Fargo fired from on his back. The bow shattered into pieces as the Pawnee went backward with the heavy slug in his gut.

Fargo pushed to his feet and heard Pepper's cry of fear and anger. He saw her, a Pawnee hanging on to her arm as she tried to pull away. He started toward her when he saw her bring one of the sacks around in an arc. She smashed it into the Indian's groin and he let out a sharp gasp of pain as he clapped one hand to his testicles and dropped to his knees. Pepper brought the other sack around as a sledgehammer of coins, smashed it against the Indian's head, and he fell sideways. Another charging figure came from the trees directly behind her, and Pepper tried to run.

"Drop," Fargo shouted.

She obeyed, her reactions quick as she went down on one knee. Fargo's shot cleared the auburn-tinted hair by a half-inch at most as it plowed into the charging figure. The Pawnee went into a stumbling, falling half-dance as he went down.

Fargo heard Joe Plum's gun erupt, two shots, and he darted a glance to the trees at his left to see a brave collapse to the ground. He paused, listened to the sound of three horses galloping away, and glimpsed one with a rider bent low on its back. The attack had been broken off, but it had only been a harbinger of things to come, Fargo knew. He reloaded, picked up the three medicine bundles, and called to the others.

"We'll circle back down to get the horses," he said, and broke into a trot.

Penny ran at his heels, the others behind her as he moved down the hillside. He turned to his left as he spotted the horses. He expected the figure that stepped into sight, bow raised, and he fired instantly. The Pawnee staggered backward and fell. Fargo reached the Ovaro, pushed the medicine bundles into his saddlebag, and swung onto the horse.

"We ride fast and hard as we can," he said. "We'd only lose time trying to cover our trail."

"You expect they'll be coming after us," Pepper said as she swung in beside him.

"I know damn well they will. We violated the sacred place. They'll be all awake and ready to ride within a few hours, I'd guess," he said. He cast an eye upward to see the first gray light of the dawn as it seeped across the sky. "Let's ride," he bit out grimly, and sent the Ovaro downhill in a fast canter.

He set a fast pace as the new sun came up to flood the mountainous terrain with light. He saved wear and tear on the horses by following whatever deer and moose trail he could find. Some wandered, took them out of their way, but all led downhill. When they reached a wide, flattened section, he drove forward at a full gallop and finally halted at the end; to the right a high ridge rose, and on the left the land dipped down. He swung from the saddle and let the horses rest. The sun told him more than two hours had gone by. He scanned the high ridge and the low land opposite, and his lips drew in grimly.

"The main part of them will be following our trail, but they'll send fast riders out ahead to spread out on all sides. They'll be catching up to us damn soon," Fargo told the others, and turned to the old miner. "You take the girls and ride down into the foothills, Joe," he said.

"Where will you be?" Penelope frowned.

"Here, waiting," Fargo said.

"You can't hold them off all by yourself," Penny said. "You couldn't even buy us much time. This is foolish."

"I don't figure to hold them off. I figure to bargain," Fargo said, and pulled the three medicine bundles from his saddlebag. "These are as sacred as the sacred place. They all hold objects that the Pawnee believe have been touched by the great spirit. I figure they'll be willing to trade our lives for the medicine bundles."

"And if you're wrong?" Pepper asked.

He shrugged. "You'll still be ahead of them. You might just make it," he said.

"No, you come with us," she said.

"Yes, no bargaining. Run with us," Penny agreed.

"Get on your horses, dammit," Fargo snapped. "This isn't up for a vote. I run with you and we're all dead. I stay and bargain, and maybe we all make it back alive."

"The man's right," Joe Plum said as he climbed onto his sturdy-legged pony.

Pepper stepped forward and her arms reached up as her mouth pressed hard against Fargo's lips. She pulled away and Penny's lips found his, a tender, lingering touch. When she stepped back, Penelope's brown curls brushed against his cheek as she kissed him, finally stepped away.

"I can't lose." Fargo grinned. "I've got my own flesh-and-blood medicine bundles. Now get the hell out of here."

He stayed beside the Ovaro as they rode away, Joe in the lead, and disappeared down the slope. Then he climbed onto the horse and made his way up to the top of the ridge. He halted there, all but silhouetted in the bright light of the sun. He hadn't waited long when he saw the two advance braves come into sight below, both riding hard, one near the ridge, the other far on the other side of the trail. They spotted him almost at once, and the nearest one sent his pony charging up the slope to the ridge. He carried a long lance in one hand, Fargo saw, and slowed when his pony crested the top of the slope. He backed a dozen paces, and Fargo saw the Pawnee's glance go to the other rider, who had come up to the ridgeline behind him. The second advance rider held a bow with the arrow drawn and ready to fire. They had put him between them and they advanced across the top of the ridge toward him.

Fargo glanced back, looked forward, and then back again. He waited, let them move closer as he drew the Colt from its holster. Suddenly, with a sharp cry, both sent their ponies into a gallop and charged him. The arrow would reach him before the lance, he realized, and he dropped over the side of the saddle, spun his body around, and fired as the Pawnee released his shaft. The Indian flew from his pony as his arrow went wild, and Fargo dived headfirst to his left and felt the lance graze the back of his shoulders. The Pawnee yanked his pony around, raised his arm, and flung the lance at the figure on the ground. Fargo tried to roll and was yanked backward as the lance tore through the shoulder of his jacket and pinned him to the ground.

The Pawnee leapt from his mount, and Fargo saw the tomahawk upraised in the Indian's hand as the man came at him. He drew one leg back and kicked out with all his strength. The blow caught the Pawnee's hurtling body in the stomach, and the Indian grunted as he fell backward. Fargo swung his arm over and yanked at the lance that held him pinned to the ground like a fly at the end of a pin. He yanked again, felt the lance loosen. One more hard pull brought it free. But the Pawnee was hurtling down at him again, the tomahawk poised to bring down. Fargo got the pole of the lance around enough to push it upward and jam it into the Indian's neck as the brave struck with the tomahawk. It was enough to deflect the blow, and the short-handled ax hit the ground beside his ear.

The Pawnee gagged, fell backward, and clutched at his throat where he'd run into the pole. He gagged again, took another step back, and Fargo swung the lance around, rose up with it, and drove it forward. His shoulders quivered as the weapon went almost all the way through the Pawnee's midsection. He let go of the lance, and the Indian fell onto his back, the lance quivering as it rose into the air, not unlike a flag-pole with the flag missing.

Fargo stepped back as he heard the thunder of horse's hooves approaching on the trail below. He swung onto the Ovaro, rode out onto the center of the ridge again, and saw the main party of the Pawnees below. They spotted him and whirled almost as one to charge up the slope. Fargo let them almost reach the top when he pulled the three medicine bundles from his saddle, held them high in the air, and put the muzzle of the Colt against the first one. The Pawnee reined to a halt only a half-dozen feet from the top of the ridge. Fargo recognized the Indian in the lead as one of the shamans. The Pawnee's eyes were black coals as he stared at the medicine bundles.

The muzzle of the Colt pressed hard against the sacred object as Fargo held the gun steady, remained silent, and let the shaman pursue his own thoughts.

The Pawnee priest spoke first. "Give us the medicine bundles," he said.

"Give us our lives," Fargo said, not moving the Colt a fraction.

The Indian's eyes were cold black fury. "We will kill you and take them," he said.

"I'll kill them first," Fargo answered, and knew his words would be understood. The Medicine bundles were real, living, throbbing with the great spirit. He pulled the hammer of the Colt back, and the click of sound was loud in the silence of the ridge.

The shaman's eyes flickered in his stern face. "You have walked in the sacred place. You must be punished," he intoned.

"The great spirit will punish us, in his way, in his time," Fargo said. "But if you let harm come to the medicine bundles, you will answer for it." He waited as the shaman wrestled with more than thoughts, fighting with the inner forces of sacredly held beliefs and burdens of earthly responsibility to his gods.

"Give us the medicine bundles," the shaman said with a hint of weariness in his voice. "You can go then."

Fargo kept the Colt against the medicine bundle. "You swear this on the powers and spirit of this medicine bundle," he pressed.

The shaman nodded gravely, his mouth a grim line. He was letting revenge go, always a hard thing to do. Fargo took the gun away from the medicine bundle, pulled the other two from his saddlebag, and held them out. The shaman urged his horse up the last of the slope, approached alone, and reached out his hand. Fargo gave the sacred objects to him and met the Indian's eyes of coal-black fire. Revenge would never be forgotten. It had been put aside for another time, the promise in the Pawnee's eyes.

Fargo stayed motionless as the shaman returned to the others and led the way down the slope to finally disappear up into the thick terrain of Arrow Mountain. The name was too damn fitting, Fargo grunted as he turned the Ovaro and rode across the ridge, suddenly aware that he was sweating profusely. He didn't hurry, followed his own paths downward, and when night came, he kept riding, halting only when fatigue overtook him.

Joe had raced hard, he knew, and he'd be camped somewhere at the end of the foothills. Fargo slept until morning and was in the saddle before the sun cleared the mountain peaks behind him.

He found a pool and enjoyed the cool, clean waters.

He knew the others had crossed into Missouri by now. He resumed riding slowly, and the day had begun to edge toward dusk when he finally reached the clay hills of the abandoned Peabody Mine once more. He took the Ovaro along the side of the hills as he approached the house, dismounted at the rear, and walked around to the front door. He knocked softly.

Pepper opened up, and her eyes grew round as pale-blue saucers as she stared at him.

"Came to collect my money," he said.

Her arms were around him, her lips on his, and he felt the warmth of her breasts through his shirt. The others were there in an instant, hanging on to him also, each offering their lips. Finally they half-walked, half-pulled him into the living room.

"We'd given up on you. We have hardly talked in days," Pepper said. "Joe went to town for supplies. He'll be back later."

"What have you decided to do, besides split the money?" Fargo asked.

"Stay here, get to know each other, maybe make the mine work again with Joe's help. If not, do something else. We've no where else to go back to, none of us," Penelope said. "But we want one thing more."

"What's that?" Fargo asked.

"We want you to stay," she said.

"For a while, maybe, only for a while," he answered, and saw the private little glances they exchanged.

"A while will do. Sisters ought to share things, I always heard," Pepper said.

Fargo's smile was slow. He'd definitely stay for a spell. As long as he could, or until his strength gave out. He had the sudden feeling that Clarence Peabody was giving a nod of approval from someplace.

*Indian Summer, 1861,
just before an effort to open the Bozeman Trail
from Fort Laramie to the Montana goldfields
brought open war in northern Wyoming.*

The dust was six inches thick on Post Street in Fort
Laramie, and a man was having his face ground into
it. Skye Fargo could hear him grunt in pain, as his
attacker lifted a heavy boot and thumped it repeat-
edly into his belly and ribs.

Initially, two others had helped pull the slender,
sallow-skinned man off his horse and batter him into
the dust. Fargo had glimpsed this gang-up as he came
downstairs from the hotel above the Rounders
Saloon, and had watched it from the hole-in-the-wall
entrance, squinting irritably, while he grew accus-
tomed to the mid-morning sunlight. He'd been on his
way to the barber's for a bath and trim, a big, tousled

man in a buckskin jacket, feeling scruffy and knowing he looked it. His lake-blue eyes were slightly bloodshot, his bearded face a little puffed, for he'd just left the bed and booze of a sweet-juicin' waitress.

Right now, though, he felt just enough twist to interfere with the unfair fight. He wedged through the gathering crowd. By the time he broke to the front, the two attackers had desisted with their victim on his knees, leaving the finishing touches to a red-haired, red-whiskered bruiser in a frock coat who, by the smirk on his thick lips, was enjoying his task.

There was something vaguely familiar about the redhead that made Fargo take a sharper look. He smiled then, coldly, recognizing that fat mouth and piggish eyes. Along much of the Oregon Trail, Tully Nickles had a mean reputation with a gun—and indeed, Fargo saw Nickles' hickory-handled Colt Navy protruding from the holster low on his thigh, rigged for a quick draw. From the Trail's beginning at Independence, Missouri, westward past Fort Laramie to South Pass in the Rockies, there was a saying that Nickles's revolver went to the highest bidder—and he'd always been busy.

"Git up, you yaller dawg," Nickles growled. "You've been paradin' around here like you're a man, so c'mon and prove it!"

Fargo glimpsed the slight bulge underneath the sallow man's coat on the left side, indicating a concealed armpit holster. The man was armed, probably with a stubby-barreled .36 or .38 caliber storekeeper's model pistol, but it wouldn't do him any good. By the time he got his hand inside his coat, he'd be a dead man. It was a mystery to Fargo why somebody wanted the man out of the way, but it was clear Tully Nickles had been selected for the job.

"Yuh ain't got a hair on your ass if you—" Nickles began. He didn't finish the sentence, his victim finally goaded by pain and embarrassment into making his fatal move. One of the gawking bystanders yelled in alarm as the man fumbled to draw, and Nickles' right hand swept to the hickory butt of his revolver.

As the Colt slid from the well-oiled holster, Skye Fargo thrust through the crowd in a flying dive. Powerful fingers gripped Nickles' wrist, forcing the weapon away from the man. It discharged with a blast, and now other onlookers shouted, this time more in fear. Fargo grinned over Nickles' shoulder, never relaxing his grip. He wrapped his left arm around Nickles' head, forearm pressed against the gunman's throat, tightening his pressure. Nickles dropped his revolver to the dust, and Fargo kicked it away with his boot, then caught him by the left arm, spun him around and smashed a heavy fist into Nickles' gaping face.

Nickles stumbled backward into the crowd. Blood trickled from his split lips as he reeled, recognition coming into his dazed eyes.

"Remember me?" Fargo asked coolly.

"Skye Fargo! Damned right I do, you bastard!"

Fargo grinned. He handed his high-crowned hat to the nearest spectator and then slipped out of his jacket. He stood out in the center of the circle, a lean and feral glint to his eyes. "Come again?"

"Comin' plenty." Nickles grunted, plunging forward, huge fists balled and hairy, hatred written across his broad face.

Fargo waited for him, eyes shifting to the two men who had been in the fight at the beginning. He glimpsed the beaten man crawl to the edge of the circle, shaking his head groggily—then his view was consumed by Tully Nickles lashing out with his right fist and trying to drive Fargo to the ground. Fargo ducked and again his hard-knuckled hand snapped out, this time catching Nickles in the bridge of the nose and breaking it cleanly. Gore gushed out as Nickles tottered onward, screaming with the pain. His two compadres had shifted positions and were coming up on either side of Fargo, the smaller of the pair—a stocky, balding man in dirty garb—diving toward Fargo's knees.

"Tackle 'im, Grady!" the other gent yelled.

Fargo danced back lightly and then brought his right foot up with all the force he could muster. The toe of his boot dug into Grady's stomach, knocking the wind from his lungs. He gasped once and then lay on his face shivering, digging stubby fingers into the dust, vomiting his last meal in a puddle under his face.

Nickles was up and full of fight despite his broken nose. Tears coursed down his cheeks as he lunged in again, while the third man, a rangy chap in tan shirt and flat-crowned teamster's hat, rushed in from the other side. Skye Fargo dodged in between the two of them as the crowd yelled in appreciation. Pivoting suddenly, Fargo charged the third man, hitting him half a dozen times in the face with fierce, lightning-like punches before stepping away to meet Nickles again.

Somewhere, somehow, Nickles had come up with a length of iron chain in his hand. Feinting as though to retreat, Fargo caused the gunman to over-extend his swing, and slipped inside its arc, ramming a fist into Nickles's unguarded belly, doubling him up. He then grabbed hold of the abruptly slackening chain, wrenched Nickles forward, and kneed him solidly in the balls. Nickles turned pale white, pawed at his crotch, and went down in a writhing heap, cursing shrilly.

Fargo tossed the chain aside and stepped back, looking at his bleeding knuckles. Nickles squirmed in the dirt, color slowly returning to his face, eyes glittering with hate. He glanced at his long-barreled revolver lying on the ground a half-dozen yards away.

"Go on, pick it up," Fargo said softly. He shifted his holster so that his Colt was positioned just so. "Go ahead, Tully."

Nickles rubbed his face with the palm of his hand. "I reckon you're gettin' into somethin' bigger than you figured," he croaked. "This wasn't your shindig, Fargo."

"I made it mine. Pick up your gun, if you got the guts."

" 'Nuther time," Nickles growled. He staggered to his feet, wavering, and shifted his glare from Fargo to the beaten man, menace heavy in his voice. "We ain't done either, Jeppson, you'n me."

The man he'd called Jeppson stood purse-lipped,

mopping his face with a linen handkerchief. His features were a little pale beneath his sallow complexion, but he was unafraid. "Another time, any time."

Fargo, chuckling derisively, scooped up the dropped revolver, and while Nickles was rousting his two pals, he shucked out the percussion caps and tossed the useless weapon to its owner. Nickles shoved it in his holster and, cupping his groin with one hand and his nose with the other, hastily barged through the crowd, sided by his wobble-legged buddies, in an ignominious retreat to the saloon.

"Thanks," Jeppson said to Fargo.

"My pleasure. Never had much use for Nickles."

"Still, he's right, it wasn't your scrap. You don't know me."

"I know him, and I've seen him work before. That's why I stepped in. Hate to say it, mister, but somebody wants you killed."

Jeppson shook his head. "Naw, him an' his pards were just a li'le drunk, is all, and feeling wringy." He was lying and Fargo knew it, although not why. Fargo didn't ask, simply shaking hands as the man introduced himself: "Mel Jeppson, commissary for Regina Express, Mister . . . Fargo, did I hear? Yes? Glad to meet you."

"Call me Skye," Fargo replied affably, turning to retrieve his jacket and hat. The big, rawboned bystander who'd held them during the fight was grinning widely; so were the other spectators as they began dispersing, noisily babbling queries and opinions.

Jeppson regarded Fargo as if deliberating, gauging

the two hundred-plus pounds of muscular frame and judging the character of the man within. Abruptly he asked, "You're not from around here, are you?"

"Nope. Just hit town yesterday, in from Nebraska way."

"Looking for work?"

"With John Bozeman, I am, but I haven't found him."

"Christ, you like living risky, don't you? Well, the latest scuttlebutt is that Bozeman's been delayed by lack of money or official permission or somesuch, and won't get here for a few months."

"Damn! I might've guessed." Annoyed, Fargo brushed back the wave of black hair that habitually fell over half his forehead, and snugged his hat down tight. "Okay, I could use a job."

"C'mon, then, I'll take you to Regina."

The bystander interrupted with a sardonic laugh. "F'get it. You got better odds of stayin' alive by trail-blazin' with Bozeman. You're a stranger, else you'd know Luther Chadwick sent out word he don't cotton to Regina, and there ain't a gent in Fort Laramie fool enough to buck him and hire on. Worse luck, them's were a couple of his Consolidated muleskinners. Chadwick won't cotton to you whumpin' 'em, extra moreso 'cause it saved Mel and that's a boost for Regina."

Fargo wasn't particularly surprised, for he was well aware of Consolidated and Luther Chadwick. Consolidated Transport ran the largest freight network in the Territory, having hundreds of skilled teamsters, prime oxen and mules, the best Murphys and newest Studebaker wagons. Owner Chadwick bossed his vast operation with an iron fist, expanding roughshod, relentlessly busting or absorbing all competition.

All except Regina. Somehow it'd managed to survive, though from the snatches of saloon gossip Fargo had overhead the previous night, Regina Express was a shoestring outfit barely holding on. It hauled just enough cargo to keep its delapidated yard open, cover the feed bill of its crowbait teams, and meet the wages of what few loyal 'skinners would still whip for it.

And pay, Fargo thought, Mel Jeppson's salary as commissary in charge of loading and supplying—and of recruiting unwary strangers by explaining little and admitting less. No wonder he fibbed! Even discounting for barroom bullshit, Regina sounded like it was in a helluva tight box, one just about the size of a coffin.

Jeppson's jaw thrust out. "Who asked you to butt in, Hoyte?"

"Now, don't get feisty, Mel," the big man cautioned with a tolerant grin. "Puttin' up a front is fine, but hell, you gotta have somethin' to back it. Instead you had that fire in your yard, you lost your last two trains, half your crew's quit, and you ain't got no wagon-masters. Everyone knows Regina's about to pack it in."

"Everyone's wrong. We are not folding," Jeppson insisted, appealing to Fargo. "See for yourself. We're getting wagons ready for another run, and need teamsters, blacksmiths, wheelwrights—"